# Storm Queen

## STORMKIN: BOOK ONE

## MARISSA DOBSON

# Dedication

To Thomas—my wonderful husband.

I'd also like to thank my wonderful editor Rosa Sophia and proofer Brynna Curry for helping me make this book stronger for it's re-release.

To my readers. Thank you for your support.

I hope you enjoy Storm Queen as much as I enjoyed writing it.

# Dedication

To Thomas—my wonderful husband.

I'd also like to thank my wonderful editor Rosa Sophia and proofer Brynna Curry for helping me make this book stronger for it's re-release.

To my readers. Thank you for your support.

I hope you enjoy Storm Queen as much as I enjoyed writing it.

# Chapter One

Kayla Benson leaned against the bar, fighting to keep her eyes open. Saturday nights were Stormie's busiest, but after one of the bartenders called in sick, forcing her to pull a double, her feet ached. Exhaustion tensed every muscle in her body, making her wish she could call it a night.

"Boss, you okay?" Trey—the bar's bouncer—came out of the kitchen, shrugging on his leather jacket. He had stayed behind after they closed, helping her lock up.

"Sure. It's just been a long night." One that wouldn't be ending for a few more hours. The bar needed setting up for the Sunday lunch crowd, and payroll waited on her desk.

*Molly couldn't have called off on a worse night.*

Instead of telling Kayla directly, she'd left a message with one of the waitresses. Tomorrow, Kayla planned to put an ad in the paper for a new bartender. The lackadaisical Molly was done for.

"You sure you don't want me to stay?" He shifted, ready to take his jacket off. "I can—"

She raised her hand, stopping him. "No, thanks though. You go home and enjoy the rest of your weekend. I'll see you on Monday."

"I don't like leaving you here by yourself." He looked dangerous, one of the main reasons she hired him, but he also had the heart of a saint. He was six-foot-five, his preference for jeans and a white T-shirt showing off his corded muscles. The rough leather jacket and motorcycle added to his bad boy persona. He was the kind of man every woman lusted over, hard and dangerous yet blessed with a heart of gold. When he cared about someone, he looked out for them.

"I'm fine." She rubbed the small of her back, trying to relieve the tension. "I've got a few hours of payroll to do yet. Not to mention orders to place."

He eyed her, one hand on the side door the staff used. "You got my number. Call me if you need anything. I'm just around the corner and can be here in a few minutes."

"A lucky woman is going to steal you away from me one day and then where will I be?" She teased. When that sad day came, she'd be at a loss. He was one of the best bouncers Stormie's ever had. "Don't worry. I'll be fine, but I have your number on speed dial." She waved him off.

He nodded and opened the door. "I checked the other entrances. Everything's locked tight. Make sure this door locks behind me and take the back steps up."

"Were you this demanding with the last owner?" Biting her tongue would have been kinder and far less careless. The former owner had been killed in the bar and she didn't need Trey's pointed look to remind her. Pushing away from the bar, she paced over to the door.

Over the last few years, Sweetwater had changed. She couldn't put her finger on what caused the transformation, but there was something different about the town where she had grown up. It had gone from being a small town with friendly neighbors to being sinister and dangerous. After dark, people didn't venture out alone unless they absolutely had to. The sun rarely shined; it seemed as if the gloom refused to leave.

The door shut and she heard him try the handle once, checking that it was secure, and a couple of minutes later his motorcycle rumbled to life.

*Payroll isn't going to do itself.* She rubbed her eyes and patted the door. All secure. The hair on the back of her neck rose and she turned to find a man standing on the other side of the bar.

"How the hell did you get in here?" She spoke the words on a harsh exhale.

"That is not imperative at the moment. You must come with me." His voice was a smooth as velvet but with a constant edge to it.

"Like that's going to happen." Covering her anxiety with a snort, she backed up to the door, wishing Trey had stayed. Adrenaline chased away her fatigue as she grabbed for the handle. "It's time for you to leave. The bar's closed."

Between one heartbeat and the next, he was in front of her. The overhead light glistened off his skin. An intangible force pushed her back against the cool metal door. Desire washed away her fear.

"Who are you?" Violent, inexplicable need harshened her tone.

"That matters not."

"It matters to me. You're in my bar after hours. I have the right to know your name."

"Nightmare."

It sent chills up her spine. "Nightmare, huh?" *Just what I need, some punk from the local gang trying to shake me down.* She looked him over. His dark gray suit cast a question on gang affiliation. *He's not the type I'd expect to cause problems for business owners. What is he into? Maybe not a gang...could the mob have moved into Sweetwater?*

"I can bring your deepest fears to life." His rich voice sent a rush of

7

heat through her body.

She raised an eyebrow in question. *Great, an escaped mental patient walks into the bar. Can this night get any worse?*

"If you don't believe me, look down." The cool dare interweaving the words drew her gaze toward the floor—and it disappeared beneath her feet.

She stood on a steel beam in the air, suspended over the town in the dark with no one there to help her. Frozen and unable to move, her heart thundered in her ears. Squeezing her eyes shut, she swallowed the hard lump in her throat. *This isn't real.* She repeated the refrain, but not even the knowledge of standing in the bar dissuaded her mind from what her eyes told it. She was a thousand feet up, panic engulfing her.

"Believe me now?" He taunted.

"Please…" *I'm going to die.* A tear escaped her clenched eyes and she peeked down again, the acrid taste of bile in the back of her throat. The floor became solid once more and she collapsed. Sucking in noisy gulps of air, she tried to reconcile the insane with the real but her mind rebelled.

"Come with me now before we are late," Nightmare ordered, his impassive visage cold and unforgiving.

"What do you want?" She choked out.

"I mean you no harm."

"No harm? Are you out of your mind?" It took everything she had not to vomit. "Get out."

He squatted in front of her, remorseless. Catching her upper arm in his hand, she thought he wanted to pull her up, but froze and instead dropped to his knees beside her, his head bowed.

Alarmed further, she watched him warily. "What is it? Are you okay?"

"Kayla, you are a Queen." His voice barely rose above a whisper. "A Stormkin Queen. The one I have searched for."

"What are you babbling about?"

"Come, let's get you off the floor and I will explain." He pulled her to her feet and helped her to a nearby booth, almost reverently. "You are a Stormkin Queen," he repeated.

"You're crazy." Maybe calling him on it wasn't the smartest move, but nothing that happened since Trey left seemed to resemble anything sane. She would have already fled if not for shakiness lingering in her trembling muscles. At least that's what she told herself. "You said that all ready, but I don't know what you mean. I've never heard of Stormkin and I'm nobody's queen."

"Stormkin is our race. We come from Shadow Providence. It's a parallel plane to your world. We are divided into territories as you are divided into states. Each territory has its own Queen, with Enforcers chosen by the Queen to carry out her rulings. Our land is similar to how your government runs, only it has harsher laws and punishments. Some rulers are unforgiving. If you disobey the command of a Queen, the penalties can be severe. Shadow Mother rules over Shadow Providence as a whole, as your president rules over your land." The tidal wave of information battered her.

"But what do you mean I'm a Queen?" Kayla debated the swiftest way out—a phone call to the police or the door.

"It was prophesized long ago. A Queen, unlike any other, would be born. She will take in the half-breeds, the unwanted, and those too dangerous for other monarchs to keep around. She'll return the Stormkins to their former glory and help defeat the Sunkins. It has been my mission to find her—you. I've searched for you my whole life. I've been sent to your realm for more than one reason but I will protect you with my life if necessary."

"I don't need to be protected," *except from you*. But she swallowed that addendum. "I'm just a bar owner. There's no need for you to lay your life down for me but you can get out of my bar."

"Forgive me your highness, but we have waited for you for so long. You'll be a safe haven for those in need, a protector for those who cannot protect themselves. We need you." He stared at her from across the booth, his gaze drilling holes into her.

Her heart began to jackhammer. *Bartender slain after being trapped with a lunatic.*

*Stay calm. Breathe. Focus. Keep him talking.*

"How can I be a Queen to the Stormkins? I'm human. I was born *here*. I didn't come from another world; I grew up just a few blocks away." *How do I get the crazy guy out of my bar?*

"You might have been born here, but you are still one of us. Your father was one of the greatest Stormkin Enforcers. He left Shadow Providence to be with your mother, who was not a Stormkin. He gave up everything for her. You have to return to our people. Many are dying, we need you." The man—*what the hell kind of a name is Nightmare?*—seemed to genuinely believe every word he spoke.

*But who is more the fool? The fool telling the tale or the fool sitting here listening to it?*

She sat there in silence for some time, staring down at the ring her father gave her on her birthday years ago. She never thought much of that day, but her father wove a fanciful story when he slipped it on her finger. *One day a man will come for you and you'll need this. It will provide you with the knowledge of who to trust. Trust in it, for though I won't be there with you, it won't lead you astray.*

Shaking free of the cobwebbed memory, she stared at the man across from her. *He couldn't…no, there was no way Dad meant this. I finally own Stormie's. My life is getting back on track. Now some guy shows up and tells me I'm from another world. This has to be some kind of cruel joke. Am I being punked?*

"But how can I help? As you said, I'm human."

"Not entirely. Your mother might not have been one of us, but the blood that runs through you is Stormkin. You have abilities you have tried to keep hidden and yet more you don't know exist. Being reunited with your people will bring on your abilities quicker than you ever thought possible. The ones you have been trying to suppress need to be set free. If any of us are going to survive, we need you to be at your strongest. We have time before we must return to Shadow Providence—to the Mother Shadow—and during that time we will need to work on your abilities."

"How can there be more than one Queen?" The memory of the ring opened her mind a little more to what he was saying. Little things about her past made it more believable and as much as she'd like to deny it, she did have one ability that came to mind. She'd hear him out before she made the decision as to whether she needed to call the men in the white coats.

"Our land is separated into many divisions with a Queen ruling her own territory. They meet four times a year, or as emergencies call for, to discuss issues that affect them all. Mother Shadow rules over each Queen. I'm here on Mother Shadow's orders. I was not given complete instructions, only that I must familiarize myself with Stormie's new owner. I must contact Mother Shadow to start the process of acquiring your territory."

*Good, an excuse to get rid of him. It will give me time to talk to Dad.*

Kayla scooted to the edge of the booth, ready to stand. "Do what you must; I have payroll to attend to."

He caught her arm. "The Stormkin people need you. Don't you comprehend that? You will need to find somebody to run the bar for you. You now have more important things to attend to."

"Excuse me, but who the hell do you think you are? You might be able to come in here, tell me I'm some Queen and I might just believe you." *Believe him?* She wasn't sure how she got to that part, but at least part of her believed him. He wasn't some escaped mental patient. There was a truth to his words she couldn't deny, especially not when she added in the small hints her father gave her throughout her life. "But you *will not* come in here and take away the bar I've worked so hard for. For years, I've put away every penny I could so that one day I could own this place. I'm not sure what it is that drew me to Stormie's, but I won't give it up now." She rose, furious, her hands balled into fists. She felt ready to take on the world, or at least the man before her.

"We require your help. You cannot turn your back on your people." Nightmare rose from the booth, looming over her. The weight of his gaze intimidated her. "People are suffering and dying while they wait for the Queen that has been prophesied."

"My people? Up until twenty minutes ago, I had no idea there was another race of people. The Stormkins are not my people. Where were they all my life? Were they around when I needed them? If Dad left them to be with my mother, why didn't he return after her death? Why did we stay here?"

# Chapter Two

"Your father abandoned his people. He is a deserter, therefore never allowed to return to his homeland. If he returns, Mother Shadow could demand he pays with his life. He knew the consequences. Instead of going to Mother Shadow, he deserted us. He left in the middle of a battle and men died because of his actions." Resentment colored Nightmare's voice and his expression hardened, harsh and unforgiving.

Kayla's mouth dropped open. She didn't want to believe it, but she could taste the truth of his words. "You were one of the men he deserted." It was more of a statement than a question. Yet Nightmare nodded.

"Yes, I was there. He thought no one would know he chose a woman over his people. I saw him sneaking through the trees on the way to the portal between the worlds. He left Dreamer and Illusion in the midst of a heated skirmish."

She reached toward him, gently laid her hand on his arm, offering comfort. As they touched, Nightmare's memories unspooled across her mind's eye. "They...they were your brothers."

His arm went stiff before he pulled back, taking his memories with him. "Yes. Triplets. I saw Illusion cut down in front of me, because your father left him surrounded by enemies without anyone to watch his back. So many good men died because of your father's actions. Dreamer's injuries nearly took him as well. His scars haunt him still. I nearly lost both of them that day. Your father cannot return. Shadow Mother will demand his life for the loss of her Enforcers."

Unease slid through her. "If I return to this…this Shadow Providence with you, will I not be held accountable for my father's actions? After all, I'm a result of his leaving."

With Nightmare standing in the middle of the bar before her, she seemed to be tumbling down the rabbit hole. No matter how surreal, she believed him. *Could Dad have really chosen love over his people, leaving people to die because of his choices? That doesn't seem like the father I grew up with.*

"You didn't make his choices and cannot be held accountable. You were not even born yet. Even if you had been, you're a Queen and Stormkin Queens are rare, especially now with our numbers dwindling. As a Queen, you will be protected. No harm will come to you. We have less than three weeks to prepare you for the next council meeting where Shadow Mother will assign you your territory. Once you have a territory, you'll have Stormkin members you must watch over and guide as well as your own Enforcers who will provide your protection."

*Oh, that's all. No worries. Just go to another world, get a territory, become Queen.* "How do you know Shadow Mother will assign a territory to me?"

"She gave us the prophecy about you. She said there would be a Queen born Earthside and she would be our saving grace. She would be the one to restore fertility to the Stormkin. By coming to Shadow Providence you restore the balance that was lost with your father's abandonment."

Although she shifted her weight from foot to foot, unable to stand still, Nightmare barely moved. Everything about his posture cried protection, readiness. He would deal with anything that came at them. He stood as if he were on guard, his shoulders squared, hands clasped in front of him while his gaze was all for her. She suspected that if the room had been crowded, he would have known what everyone was doing.

She tried to digest what he just said. *Leave?* Surely, she couldn't have heard him right. "I can't leave. This is my home, my business. My whole life is here. What would happen to Stormie's?"

A crease formed across his forehead and his eyes narrowed as if he was in deep thought. "Keenan. He can watch over Stormie's."

"Keenan?" *Does he really think I could leave my bar in someone else's hands? Someone I didn't even know.*

He pulled out a small K keychain and rubbed his thumb over the letter. "Keenan," he repeated. With a loud pop a short man appeared. "Kayla, this is Keenan."

She gasped, covering her mouth to keep from saying something that might be embarrassing as she tried to wrap her mind around what she'd just witnessed.

"Tell me what you see," Nightmare ordered her. "You won't be rude, consider this an experiment. I need to know where your abilities lie. Tell me what Keenan looks like."

Still trying to wrap her mind around the third impossible thing before breakfast, she hesitated. "He's short, maybe four feet. His skin's almost translucent, with a faint blue under glow. His ears are pointy, and his hair is a shiny shade of silver."

Nightmare nodded. "You're seeing Keenan in his true form. He's a storm elf."

"I don't know what a storm elf is, but he can't run my bar looking like that." She clamped her lips together, not amused by his stunt.

"Come, let me show you what others will see." He motioned her toward him. She folded her arms under her breasts, refusing to budge. She didn't like

15

being ordered around, especially not by someone she'd just met.

"How?"

"Your office." He led her toward the back of the bar and the little man—*storm elf*—followed.

"Why?"

"To show you."

She didn't know what that meant, yet she followed. She didn't feel uneasy in Nightmare's presence or Keenan's for that matter, but she hoped she wasn't being led to slaughter.

He guided her toward the mirror in her office with a gentle hand on her shoulder. He nodded to the reflective surface. "Look."

Keenan stood in front of them. Her gaze traveled over the little guy, taking him in one last time before studying his reflection. She couldn't believe the difference even though she saw it with her own eyes.

"What do you see, Kayla?"

"He looks human. In his early thirties, his skin is still pale but the blue under glow is gone. His reddish hair seems natural against his pale skin. The few freckles on his face gives him a friendly appearance. He also grew, he's still short for a man but now he's maybe five-foot-five. How's that possible?"

"Storm elves are a big part of the Stormkin society. For those who can afford it, they keep houses running smoothly. Keenan has experience in business and has worked for me in the past. He'll be perfect to run Stormie's. He can travel between our realms allowing him to report to you daily if you wish. Keenan can start tonight. He'll deal with your payroll, and we can deal with more important things."

"No disrespect, Keenan, but I don't know you. I can't leave my bar in the hands of a stranger and travel to another world."

"Miss, if I may speak?" The solicitous request invited her attention.

16

"Let's take this one step at a time. You have more important issues to deal with this night. Let me deal with your payroll, allowing you to focus on other things. Payroll will be completed for you by morning. We can sit down and go over the bar details once Nightmare has had more time to discuss Stormkin matters with you. I understand your concerns. I have managed many businesses over the decades; no one here will know I'm not human. Only Stormkins and Sunkins will see me as I am."

"Sunkins?" They threw these terms around as though discussions about fantastical creatures were normal. Of course, she looked to a man named Nightmare for answers, so maybe they exercised a flexible definition of normal.

"I haven't gotten that far, but you could say they're the other side of the coin."

Exhaustion weighed on her. The long day combined with the wild tale wore her out. No longer willing—or able—to just stand there, she leaned against her desk. "You're saying this boils down to good versus evil?"

"From a certain point of view, yes."

"If it is good versus evil, what side am I supposed to be Queen of?" Because the only thing lacking here was a quest for redemption.

"Again it depends on who you speak with. We would say we're the ones in the right, while the Sunkins would say otherwise. They are our opposites. For every good deed we do, they do something to destroy it. We're here to protect the humans, keep them safe from the Sunkins as well as themselves. I know legends say the contrary, referring to the Stormkin as the dark ones, evil ones, because we prefer the night. Little do they know the ones they should fear are the ones that walk in the day under the sun. Being able to walk in the sun like humans make them more dangerous, they act as if they are human…yet they're far from it."

# Chapter Three

"I must contact Shadow Mother." Nightmare followed her up the stairs into her small apartment. Living over the bar might not be for everyone, but she enjoyed the arrangement—especially tonight when neither Nightmare nor his little storm elf friend would leave.

"Phone's in the kitchen." She kicked off her sneakers. "I'm going to change out of my work clothes."

She was already heading down the short hallway toward her bedroom when he called after her. "We don't use phones. I need a mirror."

"A what?" She paused and glanced over her shoulder. Had she heard him correctly?

"A mirror. It's how we contact each other. Some have cell phones especially those who travel Earthside, but we must use a mirror to contact Shadow Mother. If you could direct me to one, I'll take care of it while you change."

*Sure, because going down the rabbit hole wasn't enough, let's go through the looking glass, too.* "There's one in the hall bathroom." She pointed him down the hall.

"Thank you." He nodded and walked away.

Continuing to her room, she couldn't get her mind off Nightmare's story. Could her father really be guilty of all he'd been accused of? He couldn't have left men to die. *Choosing love, I get that. But murder? Leaving men to die? No, there has to be another explanation.*

Her father lost so much when her mother walked out, she didn't know what he would do if he lost her, too. In her bedroom, she glanced at the bedside clock. It was after three in the morning.

*Too late to call Dad, but tomorrow…*

Stripping out of her bar clothes, she tossed them in the laundry basket and dressed in a pink and gray tank top and matching gray lounge pants with a pink stripe down the sides. She was tired, but Nightmare was still in her apartment and she had questions that needed answers.

Unsurprisingly, the man in question chose that moment to knock. "Come in."

Nightmare eased the door open and peeked inside. "I just spoke to Shadow Mother, she's sending another guard."

"You're leaving?" Disappointment surprised her. Only a short while ago she wanted him to leave.

"No. Dreamer will be here shortly, to join me in your protection. My brother and I are part of Shadow Mother's Enforcers, but for now, we have been assigned to you. Once you're established—set up in your own territory—you can decide who you want as Enforcers. We have been given permission to seek service with you if we desire, but that will be your choice. Once you have your territory, if you no longer require us, Dreamer and I will return to Shadow Mother. However, we have searched for you since we first heard the prophecy and would be honored to serve you."

Nightmare came off uptight and by the book. He reminded her of a cop on the job for too long; his eyes were stone cold, offering no hint of emotion. Yet, hidden deep beneath the surface glimmered a caring side she wanted to explore.

"Nightmare, you're welcome in my territory, or wherever, for as long as you want. The same goes for Dreamer."

"We'll see how you feel after you speak with your father. I'm sure he'll have a story of his own."

"But I saw it, I saw the whole thing." How could she explain to him what it was like when memories unspooled for her? She saw everything they did, the whole event, like a flip frame in a film. It didn't matter what her father said, it couldn't change the events she witnessed. Troubled, she sank down on the bed.

"When there's a bond sometimes people will believe any lie." He studied her. "You have a bond with your father. You love him. What he says may yet change your mind."

"Why do you think so little of me?" She twiddled with her ring again.

He stepped toward her. "It's not that I think less of you. You were raised among humans, their beliefs, bonds, and emotions are ingrained within you. I'm not naïve enough to think that just one conversation with me can change years of human beliefs. Though I do hope you'll give the Stormkins a chance."

"Why did he do it?" She couldn't decide if she was angrier at what her father did, or that he didn't explain her heritage.

"Only he can answer that, but love can make you do strange things."

"Did he have no other choice but to leave his people?"

"No. Shadow Mother would have given him choices, but he chose not to go to her. No one knew of his predicament until it was too late. We don't know why he didn't trust us. It's something I've wanted to ask him for years." He crossed his arms and stared down at her. The action drew her gaze to his broad chest.

"Well, I'm planning on asking him first thing in the morning." No question, she had to see her father. How would Nightmare react? "My father…"

"What about him?"

"I want to see him. But—"

"You're concerned I'll kill him?" His lips curved into the first smile she'd seen since he arrived.

"Killing him didn't cross my mind, though I guess it should have. After all, he did desert your people, killing your brother."

"True. Facts are facts, no matter how many years separate the events. The blood of those lost is on your father's hands. Do I want justice? Yes. Even in the midst of my deepest anger, I would not kill him unless the Shadow Mother orders it."

"You would kill him then." How could she discuss someone killing her father with such calmness? Was she turning into a monster?

"If Shadow Mother ordered his death by my hands and I did not do it, my life would be forfeit. I won't sacrifice my life for a selfish man. I'm not saying I don't have blood on my hands. I killed in the line of duty, but I have *never* killed an innocent, nor would I abandon my men." He took her hand in his. "Kayla, things are different in the Stormkin world. Enforcers must be willing to carry out whatever punishments their Queens order. We must do everything we can to protect and preserve her and other Stormkins. It's not a job I take lightly."

"You mentioned Shadow Mother. Do her orders overrule your Queen's orders?" If Nightmare served her, she wondered if she could order him never to kill her father.

"It depends on the situation. In theory, Shadow Mother rules over everything and everyone in Shadow Providence. However if her orders would do something that would get me killed by my Queen, then I can appeal her orders. For example, if you're my Queen and your father returns to our land it would be at my discretion if Shadow Mother ordered his death at my hands. I could appeal the request if killing him would destroy my place as an Enforcer in your territory. If I disobey or ignore her orders, it would mean my life." Of course, nothing in his world could be simple. Could it?

"Would you want to kill him?" She left her hand in his, soaking up the warmth of his touch. His answer could change everything.

"If you'd have asked me that years ago I would've said yes. Now that time has passed, I've come to accept what happened. Plus his actions gave us you, our Queen." A knock echoed down the hall from the front door. "That will be Dreamer." He gave a gentle pull on her hand, dragging her off the bed.

"Keep in mind, his scars are something that still make him self-conscious," he warned. "Don't pity him. It will only make him angry. Shadow Mother briefed him on who you are, bringing the memories of that day closer to the surface than they've been in a long time." Nightmare led the way down the hall.

# Chapter Four

Her small, cozy apartment had always been perfect for her. Since taking up residency, she had turned it into a home. When she moved into Stormie's she took the smaller place and planned to remodel the larger one for renting out. Renting the second apartment would give her extra income to put back into the bar. Renovations had been put on the back burner because of how busy the bar was. Now, with these two big men filling her living room, she wished she'd chosen the other place. The open floor plan usually made it seem larger than it was, but not now.

The brothers sat side by side on her white suede sofa looking uncomfortable, while she sat on the corner of the red Victorian fainting couch, watching them.

Nightmare warned her of Dreamer's scars, but he wasn't what she expected. Not that she could see much of his body. He wore a long sleeve dress shirt and jeans; for creatures from another plane, they blended in very well. The few visible scars ran from his earlobe down the side of his neck and disappeared down his collar. He seemed to favor his left arm, the same side as the scars.

*What happened to him?*

"You must have noticed your unusual abilities. Earlier you saw events through touch. Do you have other abilities you may have stifled over the years?" Nightmare asked.

"I'm human. I can't do anything supernatural." The minute the phrase escaped, she wanted to take it back. She didn't want to acknowledge any of the talents she'd concealed. Too many times during her childhood, she hadn't been able to control herself or her abilities and it only angered her father.

"Kayla." Nightmare's strict voice brooked no arguments. "You saw my memory of the past. Are you denying this?" When he said *past*, his gaze darted toward Dreamer, as if he would have chosen a different word if his brother hadn't been in the room.

Her father taught her that her differences were a bad thing. He trained her to deny any abilities and be normal. Maybe it was exhaustion or Nightmare's story or the hideously late hour, but she was tired of it all. "I can see a memory when I touch someone, especially if they're thinking about it. I've had to deny the things that made me different all my life. It's hard to change now."

"All Stormkins have abilities. Some more than others and Queens have the most, followed only by Enforcers. You have to accept your abilities in order for us to improve them. We don't have much time, so please don't make this more difficult than it needs to be. Now beyond seeing memories, what else can you do?"

"I know when someone lies to me." Without that ability, she would never have listened to his story—much less believed him.

"How?" Surprise laced his voice, another first since he'd burst into her night.

"I'm not sure how to explain it, I can taste it. If someone lies to me it's like a bitter taste almost like a copper penny on my tongue." She grabbed the red and white crocheted throw at the foot of the sofa and threw it over her legs. The blanket had taken her six months to make, but she was proud of it.

"I've seen what Nightmare can do, but what about you, Dreamer?"

"My abilities lie within dreams. I can see a person's dreams. If they're asleep I can steer their dreams in a different direction."

The time it took him to speak gave her an opportunity to study him without staring. He had the same creamy white skin as Nightmare, both of them with chestnut brown hair, and piercing green eyes. If it weren't for Dreamer's scars, it would've been hard to tell them apart.

"Like the Sandman. Are you the one to blame for my insomnia?" She meant it as a joke, but he didn't smile. He was as uptight as Nightmare, but even more distant and reserved. It would take more time to get through his outer shell.

"No, ma'am, I'm not. However if it's sleep you need I can help with that. If desired, my touch can act as a sleep aid."

"I've got insomnia, but I meant my question as a joke. My biggest problem is stress and that is no one's fault but my own."

Nightmare cut in, clearing his throat. "Speaking of sleep, Kayla, I'm sure you're tired. We can continue this tomorrow. We will rotate watch and bunk on your sofa if that's acceptable."

Grateful for the respite, she nodded. Her questions could wait. "There's a spare bedroom, no need to use the sofa. The bed is already made up. Please make yourselves at home and help yourself to anything in the kitchen." She rose and folded the throw.

Nightmare nodded and stood as well. "I'll accompany you to your room to check the windows."

"We're on the second floor." She snorted.

"To some of our enemies, it won't matter what floor you're on. Some can even fly. Tomorrow we'll need to do something about warding the building."

"Wards?" *Do I really want to know?*

He seemed to catch on to her confusion. "It's a magical spell weaved within the walls, windows, and doors for extra protection. Wards alert you if someone has been here and in some cases will keep an entity out, depending on their power." As promised, he followed her down the hall to her room and checked to make sure each window was locked. "Say what's on your mind."

She smiled and leaned against the dresser. Her mind was full and foggy all at once. "How do you know there's anything on my mind?"

"I can feel you drilling holes in the back of my head." He turned around, making eye contact with her. "What is it?"

"Dreamer. How will he react when he sees my father? Even if he doesn't accompany me later today, it's bound to happen eventually. Will he be able to handle it? You don't think he'd try to…to *kill* him or anything, do you?"

"Dreamer's temper is calmer than mine. He wouldn't kill out of anger. He'll be fine with your father. Now stop worrying and get some sleep. Dreamer and I will protect you."

Without another word, he left her. Too tired to change, she pulled the extra blanket she kept at the bottom of the bed over her, and stretched out on top of the comforter. Then she tried her best to drift away.

# Chapter Five

She woke up screaming. Pain lanced through her fingers, as if they were on fire. *What's going on?* The brothers burst through her bedroom door and scanned the room for possible threats. Nightmare held a gun while Dreamer stood behind him wielding a sword.

"What is it, Kayla?" Nightmare swept the room with a look.

"My fingers, they're burning." She spoke through clenched teeth, holding her hands out. She could see nothing, but they hurt like hell.

"Dreamer, stay out of the way." Holstering his gun, Nightmare crossed to her side, and knelt before her.

"What's going on, Nightmare?" She moaned, the pain nearly taking her breath away.

"You're coming into a new power. It will be over shortly. Dreamer's going to get on the bed behind you and wrap his arms around you. His abilities are more of a calming nature, his touch should help ease the pain." He nodded to Dreamer and the bed shift behind her.

"I don't want to compress your arms," Dreamer said. "May I pull up your shirt to expose your stomach? My touch will work better skin to skin."

For a moment, she was almost perplexed by his manners. He was so calm in the face of her pain and suffering. The thought was quickly dispelled by another shot of searing agony under her skin. "Go ahead." Another wave

29

of pain coursed through her. She let her head fall back to rest on Dreamer's shoulder, biting her lip, trying to suppress the scream threatening to break through.

He pushed the fabric up, baring her midriff. Careful not to raise it too high, he ran his hands against her bare skin. A cool and calming sensation replaced the fire racing through her. Slowly, she relaxed. Relieved, she cracked an eye open and stared down at Nightmare. "What causes your hands to burn?"

"I've heard legends about others coming into their powers. I think you'll be able to shoot lightning from your fingertips."

"Lightning, huh? That could be fun. Will it always be this painful?"

"No, but it's a hard ability to learn to control. Until you do, it won't always happen when you want it to. Maybe more than any other ability, this one will take practice."

"I don't care as long as the pain stays away." Her eyes drifted shut once again. *Shoot lighting from my fingertips. This is too bizarre…* A fresh wave of anguish tore through her.

"It will pass shortly. Just bear with us." Nightmare rubbed her leg, offering comfort.

"I can't take much more of this." Her muscles spasmed and pain blotted out her thoughts.

The sun came streaking through the windows, illuminating just how much damage her new ability could do. She lay in the middle of her bed, with Nightmare and Dreamer on either side of her, wrapped in their arms. They had spent hours helping her through the intense pain.

The worst of it seemed to have passed and she was even more exhausted than when she went to bed. The dresser at the foot of the bed had been one of the first casualties. A bolt of lightning splintered it, scorching the wood and singing her clothes. A pair of her panties hung from the light fixture above the bed, but her tiredness won out over any embarrassment and she left them hanging there.

"I think it's over." Nightmare ran his fingers along her side. They had gone for a period of time without a flare-up. Still he didn't remove his arm from around her waist, or move his body which was pushed tightly against hers.

"Good, I don't think I could go another round." She couldn't even open her eyes anymore.

"Cleaning up can wait. Sleep. We'll be right here with you, in case you need us." He didn't have to tell her twice.

Nightmare met Dreamer's gaze over the sleeping Kayla; the triplets had always been able to communicate psychically.

*She's the first person in centuries who's been able to shoot lightning from their fingertips. I wouldn't believe it if I hadn't seen it myself.* Dreamer stared at her as her eyelids fluttered in the throes of a REM cycle.

*I'm aware. Legend says she'll save our people. She'll have powers like nothing seen before; she'll bring the fertility back to the Stormkins, and restore the balance that was lost. It's why we've searched for her for so long.* Illusion had always been the leader of the trio, but when he died, Nightmare had stepped up. He worked closely with Shadow Mother, seeing her orders were carried out. His position gave him inside knowledge.

*How do you think her father will react?* Dreamer asked the question that weighed on both of their minds.

Nightmare studied the newly fledged Queen, debating what to say. *He had to expect she'd learn of us someday. Shadow Mother said it's very important she make the choice to come back with us. We can't force this upon her. She wants to go see him today...*

Dreamer's head shot up from the pillow, pain flaring in his eyes. *If you're worried about me, don't be. I wouldn't do anything to risk her; we need her. As much as I want justice, it's not worth losing her. In time, her father will get what he deserves even if it isn't from me.*

Nightmare nodded, knowing his brother spoke the truth. If Dreamer had wanted to kill him, he would've been dead years ago.

# Chapter Six

"Dad?" Kayla let herself into her father's country home.

"In here, Kayla." He called out from the kitchen at the back of the house. She set her keys and purse on the hallway entry table before making her way back.

"I'm just putting dinner on. Are you staying?"

"Not for dinner, thanks Dad. I stopped by because I wanted to talk to you. Gotta few minutes?" She stepped into the kitchen with Nightmare and Dreamer flanking her.

He nearly dropped the casserole dish when he looked past her to the men.

"I take it you remember them." Her voice was soft as she tilted her head, watching him. The vision she received from touching Nightmare flooded through her mind. Part of her had hoped that coming to see her father would make this all a dream, but his reaction confirmed Nightmare's memory.

"Nighthawk." Nightmare nodded his head as her father tried to regain control of his expression.

"I don't go by that name any longer. It's George now." He set the casserole dish on the counter and turned his attention back to her. "Why did you bring them here?"

"I need to know the truth and I need to hear it from you. You left…for

33

Mom?"

"Kayla, it's not something you can understand." Undeniable hatred etched clearly on his face as he looked from her to the men beside her.

"Dad, I'm not a child anymore. Please don't treat me like one. I need to know what happened." She took a seat at the kitchen bar.

"You don't need to know anything except to stay the hell away from them." He transferred his gaze to the men. "I want them out of my house."

She bounced back to her feet. "Fine, we'll leave. I don't know why I expected you to be straightforward with me on this; you never have been before, no matter the topic." The men followed her out of the kitchen, but she could see Dreamer struggled. He had something he wanted to say, but he held back. *What could it be? Did it have to do with the desertion, or Illusion?*

Her fingers closed around her keys when her father came into the hallway. "Don't go with them. No matter what they say."

"Why?" At his stony silence, she shook her head. "You'll always be my father no matter what you've done, and I'll love you. Why you won't tell me what happened is beyond me. But I have to make my own choices. Either way I've hired a bar manager and will be taking some time off. I'll be in touch when I can." With that, she marched out the door. If her father wouldn't be straightforward with her, then she was left trusting Nightmare, Dreamer, and her instincts. In less than twenty-four hours, they'd showed her more compassion than her father ever had.

They followed her to the pale blue SUV without a word. Sliding into the driver's side, she looked at Nightmare who sat in the passenger seat. "How do we get in touch with Keenan? I want him to take over the bar effective immediately."

"We'll contact him back at your apartment."

Dreamer leaned forward and put his hand on her shoulder. "Are you okay?"

She made eye contact with him through the rearview mirror, touched that he'd asked. "I'm fine." She reached up and put her hand on top of his. "Thanks."

He nodded before leaning back.

"Does that mean you'll return to Shadow Providence with us?" Nightmare inquired.

"I guess it does. What do we need to do?"

"Once we instruct Keenan about taking over the bar, I'll contact Shadow Mother to inform her of your decision. Over the next few weeks, we'll need to work on your abilities and refine them, giving you better control and accuracy. We'll go over Stormkin history, making you familiar with our people and customs. Some of it you will have to learn some of that as you go. There are also some key points we need to go over when dealing with the Sunkins."

While he spoke, she steered the SUV toward the bar. "Sounds like we'll be busy."

Dreamer chuckled behind her. "Nightmare will do his best to always keep you busy. The biggest thing we need to work on is your lightning and any other ability that pops up."

"I want to be prepared, so busy is good. I'll do whatever I need to be ready, but I'm nervous."

"Nothing to be nervous about. It will be great to have you among us. Before long it will begin to feel like home." Nightmare watched out the window as she drove back to downtown Sweetwater.

Turning onto Main Street, the flashing lights caught her attention. Police at Price's Drugs. *He must've been robbed again. What happened to the town I grew up in? Will things ever be the same again?* "Are the Sunkins to blame for

Sweetwater's change?"

"Partially. Expect more change in the coming months. Coming to Shadow Providence with us will shift the balance to where it's supposed to be."

Kayla curled up on the sofa with a cup of coffee in her hand. She tried and failed to suppress a yawn; the lack of sleep was catching up with her. Not to mention her body was sore from wriggling in pain for hours, and her headache was worsening. She needed a hot shower to help relax her muscles.

The shockingly blue-skinned Keenan stood before her, waiting.

"If you're still willing I'd like you to take over as bar manager until further notice. You'll need to replace the evening bartender, Molly. I've already dealt with letting her go, but you need to put an ad in the paper, or however you want to do it."

"Ma'am, does that mean you'll return to Shadow Providence?" Enthusiasm filled the inquiry.

"Yes." The answer made her wonder, for the hundredth time, what it would be like. Would she be happy there? If not, could she return? Would she have to do what her father did, and abandon the Stormkins?

"Your bar will be in good hands," Keenan assured her, interrupting her thoughts. "Well, I'm sure you have lots to do." He reached into his pocket and pulled out a small K keychain, similar to the one Nightmare possessed, and handed it to her. "Anytime you wish to reach me, just run your fingers over the K and call my name." With that, he was gone.

"Don't worry, Kayla, your bar couldn't be in better hands." Dreamer joined her on the sofa.

"I'm not worried about the bar. I brought it back from the dead before. I'm sure I could again if I had to. I'm just wondering what Shadow

Providence is like. If I'm not content there…what happens?"

He placed his hand on her leg. "It's unlike anywhere else. Each Queen runs her own territory, and each is different. You'll remake your area in your own image. You don't have to live under someone else's thumb."

"You didn't answer my other question. What if I'm not happy there?"

Nightmare, who remained quiet while she spoke with Keenan, leaned forward. "You don't have to stay if you're unhappy. But we would do whatever we could to see that you are."

"Why the gloom, Nightmare?"

"You don't understand what you mean to our people. I hope that you'll comprehend it when you meet Shadow Mother and see our home." He rose from the chair. "I must contact Shadow Mother."

When they were alone Dreamer took her hand. "My brother has been searching for you for years. His desire to find you only increased with Illusion's death. He can seem hard at times, but that's because of our former Queen. She was cruel and he had it worse than any of us. Give him time and you'll see another side of him. It's truly an honor for us to serve you. It would be a privilege, especially for Nightmare, if you wish to keep us on as Enforcers once your territory has been assigned you."

"I told him before you arrived that both of you are always welcome wherever my territory is." Nightmare returned, tension shimmering the air around him. "What's wrong, Nightmare?"

"Shadow Mother…" He ran his hand through his hair pushing it away from his face. It was the first gesture of unease he demonstrated in their short acquaintance. "We have seventy-two hours before we have to return."

"What?" Dreamer asked. "The next council meeting isn't for another few weeks."

"Shadow Mother has moved it up. It will be this weekend, but she requires our presence before then. She wants to meet with Kayla before the others arrive."

"What does all this mean? Why are you upset about it?" Kayla glanced back and forth between the brothers.

Nightmare circled the sofa. He didn't sit with them, but at least she didn't have to strain her neck to see him. "I wanted more time to work with you. To give you time to adjust to your new status. It also puts more pressure on you…to make a decision."

"A decision on what?" She set aside her coffee.

"Us…Shadow Mother wants an answer once we arrive if you want us as Enforcers."

"Why so soon?" Dreamer inquired.

"Kayla has a long road ahead of her, which will not be easy. Many of the legends say there will be an uphill battle for her and her Enforcers. Shadow Mother doesn't want us to get wrapped up in something we won't be able to finish. She feels we don't need to make any additional enemies." His jaw was set and he avoided eye contact with her.

"I have two questions. If I didn't want you as Enforcers, what happens? The second question, what do Enforcers do?"

"We would return to Shadow Mother, at least for now," Dreamer explained. "She was generous enough to take us in after the problems with our last ruler. The first duty of the Enforcers is to protect their Queen, then they're supposed to carry out her orders. Normally the Queen has a group of elite Enforcers whose only duty is to protect her and other Enforcers deal with everything else."

Kayla's gaze darted to Nightmare, who paced the small living room. "To take you on as Enforcers, I have to know what happened with your previous Queen. What took you to Shadow Mother?"

The brothers shared a long look before Nightmare nodded. Dreamer sighed. "After Illusion died, things were pretty chaotic, both with us and with all Stormkins. Illusion was the calming force for our team and when he died, Queen Shower—our former Queen—punished us when anything went wrong. She blamed me for Illusion's demise, but Nightmare challenged her, bringing her wrath down on him. She nearly killed Nightmare before Shadow Mother intervened."

"Is she still in power?"

"No, I killed her." Nightmare came to stand in front of the fireplace. "No Queen will take a chance on us now, afraid the same will happen to them. Shadow Mother was our only hope. Without her, we would have been exiled from our homeland. But now we have you…"

Tension cramped her stomach. They could choose what they knew over her, a wild variable. But she wanted them to choose her. Instinctively, she knew they would protect her and wouldn't turn against her.

"If given the choice, who would you like to serve? Would you rather stay where you are, or vow your loyalties to me?"

"You," Nightmare said, his tone firm. "As I told you before, it would be an honor to serve you."

"You, Dreamer?"

"I wish to serve you as well."

"I'm not sure I can live up to your expectations, but you can tell Shadow Mother I've claimed you as my Enforcers."

Both men exchanged a glance, not bothering to hide their immediate relief. Kayla bit her lip, clenching her hands together in her lap. She hoped she'd made the right decision. More than anything, she prayed she was ready for whatever was ahead.

# Chapter Seven

For hours, Kayla practiced her newfound lightning ability in the empty apartment, and nothing happened the way she wanted it to. Nightmare brought different—replaceable—objects over for her to aim at, but instead there were enough holes in the wall to resemble Swiss cheese. "Enough. I can't do this."

"You're not concentrating." He hovered like a firefighter overseeing a controlled burn, cautious and wary.

"You make it sound so easy. I'm trying but it's not helping. I can't even aim at that little pillow, how am I supposed to aim in battle?" She waved her hand toward the pillow, anger coursing through her. Dammit, she was trying. She couldn't help it if her aim was off. The cotton flying around the room startled her.

"You did it."

"But how?"

"You'll have to tell me. What were you thinking, feeling, when it happened?" He demanded.

She looked at the demolished pillow, still stunned she was able to hit *anything* other than the wall. "Anger. I was angry for not being able to do this. I can shoot a gun and hit my target exactly where I want to, but I can't do this."

"Until you master this ability, use anger to trigger it. Try the other pillow." He stood off to the side, out of her way in case things backfired.

She let the anger build inside her, forming a ball in the center of her stomach, before she raised her hand to aim. She uncurled her fingers, bringing the pillow into her sight, and forced the anger toward the pillow. Again, cotton exploded.

"There you go. If you do that, you'll gain more control over time. We'll continue practicing, but now there are some other things we should go over. Let's return to your quarters and we'll begin your history lesson over lunch." He offered her his hand.

She looked around the room, from the holes in the wall to the destroyed pillows. Would she be able to do it if her life depended on it? Her control needed to be better.

Placing her hand in his, a current ran through her from the coolness of his touch. "There's something different about the way you feel. Not different since you arrived, but different than humans." *Humans. Do I not consider myself a human anymore?*

"Stormkins are always cool to the touch."

"I meant the electricity."

The words stopped him in his tracks and he stared at her. "You feel that?"

"Sure I do. What's the big deal?"

"Do you feel it with Dreamer as well?" They started walking again, but he never looked away.

"I don't know. I can't say I paid attention."

"Let's find out." He opened the door to her apartment. "Dreamer."

Dreamer, who stayed in her apartment to clean up the mess in the bedroom, met them in the living room with a large black trash bag. "How's she doing?"

"Anger is her trigger, but she shall gain better control with time. Touch Kayla, bare skin only."

"Excuse me?" Dreamer's brows knitted together in confusion.

"Place your hand on hers," his brother repeated.

Dreamer set the bag down and placed his hand over hers, his gaze traveling between them. The same low current of energy sizzled through her.

"What do you feel?" Nightmare asked.

"It's there. What's the big deal?"

"What's there?" Dreamer's frown deepened with every passing moment.

"Electricity…it's the best way I can describe it." She wasn't sure how to explain what she didn't understand herself.

"It can't be." Dreamer eyed Nightmare as if looking for his confirmation.

"Dammit! Will one of you please tell me what the hell's going on?" She hated being so in the dark about everything. New worlds, new powers, new rules—all of it.

"When it comes to Queens, our culture doesn't believe in one man and one woman. They are not monogamous. A Queen can and often does have active partners with any number of men."

"You've got to be kidding me." She pulled away and retreated to the sofa. "Why would they need more than one man?"

"Because of our dwindling numbers it's more important than ever for our rulers to reproduce. The more men with her, the better the odds. It is her right to have any unmarried men in her territory."

She couldn't believe what she was hearing. *Do they expect me to whore myself out? Because if so, they've got another thing coming.* "I don't understand what this has to do with anything."

"The electricity you feel in our touch is proof we would make a fertile couple," Nightmare stated matter-of-factly.

"I won't become a whore." She shook her head, appalled by the suggestion.

"No one is asking you to, I'm telling you of our culture. If it's rumored there are no men in your bed once you have your territory, Shadow Mother can demand you bed one or more. Otherwise, you may lose your land. This is true with you more than any other Queen."

"Why me?"

"Our fertility will only be restored to our people once you have birthed a child."

"Nightmare, you can't be serious. Why'd you wait to tell me this?"

Dreamer knelt in front of her. "I, better than any Stormkin, know your culture as well as my own. I know it seems barbaric to you, but it's true. We hesitate only because we know where you've been raised. It's more likely to be demanded of you because our race could die if fertility is not restored. Humans will be in more danger than ever if that happens. The Sunkins will have free reign over the humans."

"What happens when I have a child? Will that be it?" *Or will you pull out some crazy task for me? Hi Kayla, you're a prophesied Queen. Oh, by the way your father is a traitor. Whoops, forgot to mention you need to let us stand stud so you can breed some heirs.* The thoughts tumbled one after another through her mind.

"As long as the couple remains fertile, she can be as monogamous as she chooses. If a royal couple has tried for more than two years without another child, the Queen will bed a selected group of men," Dreamer explained.

"If there are multiple men does a Queen never marry? How does she get her King?"

Nightmare stepped closer to her. "She may marry the father of the first child and the marriage will remain valid as long as there is fertility between the pair. Stormkins have no Kings. Women rule all territories in Shadow Providence and the men are the protectors, the Enforcers. Some will take advice from their royal consorts and Enforcers, but the Queen has the final say."

"What happens if no more children are produced?"

"After two years he must step aside, he would no longer be her spouse. Once he's no longer her spouse or royal consort he's no longer protected as one. In our land once a Queen has made love with a man and there's a possibility of a child, he's a royal consort, and is protected because he might be fertile. He may battle to protect his Queen and his own, but he cannot be challenged by another Enforcer for his place within the community."

"This is insane." Shooting lightning from her fingertips, the ability to sort through lies and find the truth, and now she had to be *bred* to give them a heir. It was too much to comprehend. It made her question, *Is Santa Claus real too?*

Dreamer placed his hand on hers, squeezing it gently. "I know this comes as a shock and it's very different from your world—"

"Different? It's unnatural, lewd, and cruel. What about love?" She wondered how they could accept such a barbaric lifestyle. Didn't anyone challenge these things?

But they offered her no other explanation; it was the way of their world. *My world.*

# Chapter Eight

Dreamer went in search of what he called essentials for the council meeting and Kayla took the opportunity to relax in front of the fireplace. Tranquil evenings at home were few and far between for her. Maybe in Shadow Providence things would be different, but somehow she doubted it.

"You've been quiet, what's on your mind?" Nightmare's calm voice twined through her like silken thread. Despite their activities, his dark suit remained immaculate.

She studied his rich green eyes, they were dark and mysterious like a forest at twilight. His long, chestnut brown hair—she just wanted to sink her fingers into the length. No use denying her attraction. It sizzled through her, almost from the beginning. She marveled over the idea they'd supposedly make a fertile couple. She didn't want to sleep with a man just to produce an heir. It wasn't fair to him, to her, or any baby they conceived.

*Besides, am I really ready to be a mother—much less qualified?*

"I don't want…" She paused, uncomfortable with the idea, with the words she was about to speak. "I don't want to sleep with multiple men…one is more than enough for me."

"If Shadow Mother hears you say that, she'll make sure you sleep with your share of men to gain your territory," Nightmare warned.

"I'd rather be *without* territory than forced into an orgy."

"Don't say that." He reached over to take her hand. "You would not survive without your own territory. The other Queens would see you as a threat and without your own Enforcers you would be an easy target."

"A threat to what?"

"Kayla, you'll have abilities beyond anything we've seen before. Another Queen would see you as a rival—as they see Dreamer and I—and would kill you to end the potential threat."

She let her head fall back to rest on the sofa. *Maybe going to Shadow Providence is a mistake. Sounds like I'll be in more danger there than I ever would be here.*

"You're doubting your decision," Nightmare stated as if he could read her mind.

She squinted at him. "Maybe. It's too dangerous for me."

"No, it's not. You'll be safer there than anywhere. Come here." He grasped her hand, and pulled her gently into his lap. "I'll show you just how wonderful it can be."

"Why do I need to be on your lap for that?"

He gave her cocky grin. "I wouldn't normally do this, but putting your fingers on my temples will give you more of a direct line to my memories. I must warn you, you'll have to take the good along with the bad. I'll do my best to shield you from the worst. Are you ready?"

She nodded and touched her fingertips to his temples. The connection crackled to life; images began to appear behind her eyes as if she were watching a movie. A small town, with shops lining cobbled streets, each one decorated for Christmas. The dark town seemed cheerful. Kids played in the streets having a good time. People gathered in groups talking and laughing; it reminded her of what Sweetwater was like a few years ago. Everyone seemed to know each other, and a bond existed between the people she saw.

The image shifted and she saw a room filled with mostly women. She knew they must be the Stormkin Queens from the way they were dressed. One drew her attention more than the others. She had on a long black gown, her dark brown hair with slivers of gray tied back in a stiff twist. She tried so hard to look stern, but underneath it there was a softness. Kayla recognized her—or maybe it was Nightmare, but she knew the regal woman was Shadow Mother. None of the other women mattered; Shadow Mother captured her attention.

Before she could take it all in the scene changed again. This time to an argument. A short woman with fiery red hair held a whip, short metal pieces at the end of each lash. Dreamer lay on the bed, his back covered in raw, bloody wounds. Nightmare screamed at her, but the only thing Kayla caught were the words "...the last straw..." before he attacked the woman, knocking her to the floor.

Nightmare tore her hands away from his head before she could see anything more. He set her aside and rose, retreating to the window.

Confused by the images and more than a little sickened by Dreamer's injuries, she could almost feel the barrier erecting between Nightmare and her. Rising, she crossed the room to stand at his back.

"Nightmare."

He continued to stare out the window not bothering to look at her. She touched his arm, and he went stiff under her fingertips.

"How can you bear to touch me when you saw what I'm capable of?"

"Nightmare..." When he tried to slip away, she squeezed his arm tighter. "I already knew you killed Shower, I don't hold that against you. Seeing it made no difference." She paused considering her next words carefully. "Maybe it did a little, but not in the way you're worried about. If anything, it gave me more understanding of why you chose to act as you did. Don't turn away from me, pushing me away will do neither of us any good. We need each other."

He looked sideways at her, staring into her eyes. "I don't want your pity."

"I feel sadness for what you and Dreamer have suffered, but not pity. I believe that everything we go through makes us who we are, and places us where we need to be. Without what you've been through, you wouldn't be here now, and I wouldn't change you being here for anything."

Fighting uncertainty, she leaned up and placed a timid kiss on his cheek.

# Chapter Nine

Kayla was packing the clothes she wanted to take when Dreamer returned with more shopping bags.

"What did you get now?"

"After I cleaned up your exploded dresser, most of the stuff in it had to be pitched—scorch marks. I went out and bought replacements, as well as things more suitable for Shadow Providence." Dreamer set the bags on the floor by the suitcase.

"Suitable, huh? What's wrong with my clothes?"

"The council meetings are more formal. You can't show up in jeans. Shadow Mother prefers formal full length dresses for these meetings." He reached into one of the bags and pulled out a long blue dress, with a beaded design around a scooped collar. There was something sexy about a man who went out and shopped for her, especially since the dress looked to be her size. Dreamer had exceptional taste in women's clothing.

"Aww, I can see what you mean by suitable. In my defense, in my line of work, dresses aren't practical." She reached into the bags examining each garment before folding it and placing it in the suitcase.

"Understandable, but I wanted you to be prepared. Tomorrow, we'll want to impress Shadow Mother." There was a touch of hesitation in Dreamer's voice, almost as if he didn't want their time here to end.

"Speaking of tomorrow, where's Nightmare?"

"He's down in the bar with Keenan, going over a few last minute things, and giving him your spare apartment key. He'll be staying here to give the impression that he's human, as well as to oversee the renovations."

"Renovations?" Why would he get someone to begin work at Stormie's without consulting her first? She didn't have the extra funds to do renovations, especially now that she had to hire Keenan.

"Oh, Nightmare didn't tell you?"

"No, but you will."

"There'll be times that we'll return to Sweetwater. Nightmare thought it would be best to have the renovations done on the other apartment. It would give us a place to stay when we're here on duty, as well as a place for you to visit your father."

"My father…" At the mention of her father, she rubbed the ring on her finger. "I don't know if he'll want to see me again."

Dreamer placed a finger under her chin, and urged her head up to look at him. "Your father will come around. Don't give up on him."

She smiled at him, unsure she really believed it. Her father could hold a grudge like no other. "I don't have the money now for the renovations. Everything I've had was put into the bar, which is just starting to turn a profit."

"No worries. As a Stormkin Queen, you have money as well as businesses in your territory that will bring in a profit. Kerry, Keenan's sister, is doing some of the work. She'll see to the design, while a professional company does the manual labor. Kerry isn't paid in your currency. Nightmare mentioned Kerry would have plans for you to see today. I thought he would have done it earlier. I'm sorry."

"It's fine. Let's finish packing and then I'll deal with Nightmare."

They still had one suitcase left to fill when the front door closed.

"Where's everyone?" Nightmare called.

"Looks like I won't have to hunt him down," she teased, tossing a sweater into the suitcase. When Nightmare entered the bedroom, she put on her best angry face before turning around to meet him. "What's this about renovations?"

Nightmare shot Dreamer a menacing look. "It was *supposed* to be a surprise. I have two design options for you to look over. Did the big mouth tell you the reason for the renovation?"

"Yes, he said because we'll be here occasionally. Now let's see the plans." She held out her hand, eager to see what Kerry had come up with.

"The first idea keeps the place similar to is the way it is now, opening it up more, then updating the kitchen and bathrooms. While the second one— my personal favorite—would be to open the two apartments making it one large space. This would give us more room and better protection. It's also more suitable to what we need for a number of reasons. The two biggest being the number of people that will be traveling with us for your protection as well as for other duties. Second, as one of your Enforcers, I wouldn't allow you to be here with a human renting the second apartment. It would be unsafe."

"I like the idea of opening it up, especially when there are people traveling with us. But it would be mostly empty while no one is here."

"Keenan would be staying here as long as he's the bar manager, so he'll need his own room no matter which option you choose."

She looked down at the plans again. Opening the two apartments would give them seven bedrooms; she assumed that would be more than enough room, even with Keenan occupying one. The large living room would run across the front of the building, taking advantage of the views of the town, as well as Sweetwater Lake.

"Let's do option two. Seven bedrooms seem like too much space, but I love the idea of opening it up and enlarging the living room."

"You'll be surprised how cramped it will feel when we're all here." Dreamer looked over her shoulder at the plans.

"What do you mean? Wouldn't it just be us?"

"Dreamer, let Kerry know which design she chose. Keenan can pass on the message if she's already left and I'll explain things to Kayla." Nightmare continued to stare at her for a few minutes after Dreamer shut the door behind him. For the first time since he arrived, uneasiness threaded through her.

"What?" She fought the urge to fidget under his watchful gaze.

"Sit down." When she just stood there, he sighed and continued. "I told you before that each Queen has Enforcers. Dreamer and I are your first, but we won't be your only. You'll need to choose an Enforcer in Charge. He'll be in charge of your protection, he'll assign guards their duties, training, recruiting, and so on. Mostly your elite Enforcers will be in charge of your security, there are normally six to twelve. Those elite Enforcers will travel with you at all times. If the threat is high there will be even more."

"Are you seriously saying I'll have an entourage every time I go somewhere? I don't want people following me everywhere I go."

"You'll always have Enforcers with you, more when you're traveling, during meetings both with Stormkins and the council. You are Queen…Queens have protection. Without Enforcers you could be in danger, *especially* you."

"What do you mean especially me?" She sank onto the bed, afraid she wouldn't like his answer.

"You have been a thing of legend for years. Some will see you as a threat. Some will fear what you'll bring and therefore try to stop you by any means necessary."

"You mean they'll try to kill me." Swallowing the lump in her throat, she looked up at him.

"It's a possibility, yes. Dreamer and I, as well as any other Enforcers you bring on will be there to protect you. It might not be the time and I know you might not trust us yet, but I would suggest either Dreamer or I as your Enforcer in Charge. We can advise you of Enforcers that would be beneficial to your protection, as well as instruct new Enforcers on where they stand from the beginning. It would also give you protection at the upcoming council meeting, as well as with Shadow Mother. Only your Enforcer in Charge can accompany you during the council meetings."

"I never imagined I'd be in danger from other Stormkins, let alone threatened by other Queens and Shadow Mother. Will I even survive in Shadow Providence?" *Tell me again why I'm doing this…*

"I'll see to it." He stepped forward, taking her hand in his, and their gazes locked while he made his vow. "I won't let anything happen to you, Kayla."

She wanted to believe him, but some things were out of anyone's control. Her life had spun wildly beyond the boundaries of sanity in just two short days. Going to Shadow Providence was a bad idea.

She knew it.

# Chapter Ten

She stood before the mirror taking another look at the dress, her hands shaking, and her stomach doing flip-flops. *What am I doing?* In the early morning hours her courage fled, leaving her to stare at the ceiling unable to sleep. Meeting Shadow Mother stressed her more with each passing moment.

"Kayla," Nightmare called from the doorway. "We should be on our way."

She eyed him through the reflection of the mirror. "I want you as my Enforcer in Charge."

"Are you completely sure? Assigning your Enforcer in Charge is not something you should take lightly. Your decision cannot be easily changed if you have second thoughts. Demoting an Enforcer, especially your Enforcer in Charge, will be seen as a weakness that can be exploited."

"I'm sure." She spun around to face him. "Are you sure I'm doing the right thing? Maybe I should stay here."

"It's your choice. It has always been your choice. Will you be happy not knowing what you could have had? Shadow Providence can give you things you would never have here. Yes, there are trade-offs. But there are trade-offs with anything important."

"All right, let's do this." She ran her hand down the front of the dress again, smoothing invisible wrinkles.

"You won't regret this and we can come back anytime you want." He stepped out of the doorway, giving her enough room to pass.

Things would be different when she returned. The two apartments would be opened into one, Kerry's ideas called for replacing most of her things and decorating. She only hoped it would still feel like home.

In the living room, she slid her purse over her shoulder, and reached for one of the suitcases. Dreamer stopped her. "No, I've got them."

She nodded, knowing it was better than arguing with him. "Dreamer, I've ask Nightmare to be my Enforcer in Charge."

He nodded, relieving her fears that he might be disappointed if he wasn't chosen. "There's no one better. Congratulations, you deserve it," he told his brother, the sincerity clear in his voice.

"We must be on our way. Shadow Mother is expecting us soon." Nightmare was all business.

The anxiety started to take hold again. "Let's do this before I lose my nerve."

Dreamer grabbed the two suitcases sitting by the door. "The portal is behind the bar. I'll take your suitcases and go first. You'll follow with Nightmare. Until you understand the portal, let Nightmare guide you."

"The portal will transport us to wherever you need to go in Shadow Providence," Nightmare explained. "All you have to do is think of the territory, visualize it in your mind, and you'll be there within seconds. This time we'll use it to go to Shadow Mother's but in future we can use it to go to and from your territory as well." They made their way down the back steps to the door that led to the alley.

In the alley, she could see nothing, but Nightmare stopped. "Here?"

"Focus with more than your eyes and you'll see it. Open up your senses." Nightmare squeezed her hand. "*Focus.*"

She did as he asked, closing her eyes for a moment, and when she opened them it was there. She could see a swirling silver doorway off to the side of the alley, resembling a quickly rotating vortex.

"What would happen if a human stumbles upon it?" She asked, concerned her bar staff might fall down the rabbit hole.

"The portal wouldn't react to a human. They would need to have our blood running through them, only then would it be visible. Then they would still need to know what they were looking for and how it worked." Nightmare gave a brief nod to Dreamer who stepped through the portal. "You don't know what to visualize so we'll go together. Just hold my hand and whatever happens don't let go or you could end up anywhere."

He took a step forward, drawing her with him. She took one final deep breath, as if she was worried she wouldn't be able to breathe, and let him lead the way. It felt as if she was being swept down a drain as the swirling silver rotated past her, and it was over before she could gather her bearings.

A small woman was waiting for them when they arrived. "Shadow Mother's expecting you. She's in the library. Leave the suitcases here and follow me."

"Ginger, it's nice to see you again." Dreamer placed the bags on the marble floor while Kayla reeled where she stood. She barely heard a word. The sensation of traveling through the portal left her feeling lightheaded, though Nightmare assured her it would only last a few minutes and she would get used to it over time.

He steadied her while she tried to stay on her feet. "Ginger is Shadow Mother's storm elf. She acts as her personal assistant and butler," Nightmare whispered in her ear, his arm tight around her waist.

"Come. We mustn't keep Mother waiting."

Kayla's heels clicked as she walked. Beautiful pictures lined the walls and antiques decorated the house, which was surprisingly warm and inviting. Maybe Shadow Mother wouldn't be as intimidating as Kayla feared. As they neared the end of the hall, Nightmare dropped his arm from her waist. Both men took up a position on either side of her, squared their shoulders, and stiffened their spines, their gazes straight ahead.

*They're on guard.* Sucking in a deep breath, Kayla tried to quell the shaking inside her. Ginger opened the door and admitted them to a private office. The regal woman from Nightmare's memories sat behind a large mahogany desk.

"I appreciate you being on time." Shadow Mother put aside some papers she was reviewing and rose. Circling out from behind the desk, she motioned Kayla to follow her to the fireplace. "Come, sit. Ginger, please bring us four bottles of Hurricane." Nightmare and Dreamer took the sofa that sat between the two chairs, making it clear she was to take the chair on the side of Nightmare.

She sat, wishing she were closer to her men. She could use the comfort, their masculine scents that had become so familiar in the last two days— anything to put her nerves at ease.

"Welcome to Shadow Providence, it's a pleasure to have a legend among us. You'll have a long demanding road ahead of you, but in the end, you'll make our land a better place, in turn protecting *humans*. I have been informed you've accepted Nightmare and Dreamer as your Enforcers, correct?"

"Yes." She didn't like the way the woman said *humans* as though the term itself was distasteful enough to sour her tongue. "They've been a great help over the last few days."

"Very well then, they can help you adjust to your new territory. After much consideration, I've canceled the council meeting. You have enemies in the land and if given the chance they would try to eliminate you. Postponing the meeting until you've had time to adjust and gather your own forces to keep you safe is the best course of action. If I step in and protect you, even at a council meeting where there's to be no danger to any of the Queens, it would be seen as a weakness. If you're to survive and complete all that has been prophesied you will need to stand on your own feet, and have Enforcers to protect you. The next meeting will be in three months." She paused when Ginger returned and set a tray with four bottles on the table.

"That's all for now, Ginger." Shadow Mother reached for one of the bottles. "Help yourself. Hurricane is one of the Stormkins' special drinks, it would compare to wine in your land. We bottle it because many Queens and elite Enforcers must be concerned with the possibility of a threat on their lives. The air tight seal allows for peace of mind."

The men each reached forward and grabbed a bottle. At Nightmare's subtle nod, Kayla selected one. The hiss of the bottle's opening filtered through the thick fog of silence in the room. Shadow Mother gave them a moment to drink before leaning forward to focus on her.

"Now, down to business. I have assigned you the Storm Hollow territory."

She heard one of her men suck in a deep breath—she could've sworn it was Dreamer—but the reason behind it escaped her.

"Shadow Mother, it's not my place to judge, but are you sure that's the wisest place to put her?" Nightmare eased forward on the sofa.

"It is *not* your place to question me. It's where she needs to be. Safety…well, that's your burden not mine." A spark of anger flared to life under her well-mannered words.

"I apologize. It's only my concern for her safety that prompts me to speak."

"Your concern is commendable, if misplaced. She will have enemies everywhere."

She might've modernized her home and appearance, but there was something that let Kayla know Shadow Mother was older than she looked...*much* older.

"I feel as though I'm missing something." Kayla finally spoke up.

"My child, you are. It's Nightmare's story and I'll let him explain it. I must attend to something. We'll have dinner together, and then you may make your journey." With that, the woman simply left. Kayla stared after her—because neither she nor her welcome were at all what she'd expected.

Minutes ticked by as Kayla waited for Nightmare to explain, but he said nothing. "Are you going to tell me what I missed or not?"

He rose and stalked over to the window unable to face her. "Storm Hollow is where I killed Queen Shower."

She didn't know what to say. Where she died wasn't as important as the people who'd been left behind—and their reaction to the men Kayla chose as her Enforcers.

"The people there...will they see us as the enemy?"

"Kayla, one thing I love about you is that you cut right to the heart of it. Most there, at one time or another, had been at the receiving end of Queen Shower's punishments, and were supportive of what happened. But she wasn't without her own allies and those are the ones we must concern ourselves with." He looked out the window to the surrounding grounds of the stone mansion they stood in. "We'll have to go in and do a complete shakeup. Any Enforcers that supported her will be no good to us. Identifying them, removing them from their duties, or exiling them to another territory can help eliminate problems before they arise. We must go in with a strong plan and show you're in charge. Any signs of weakness will give them the doorway needed to tear you apart. You'll have to trust Dreamer and I or none of us will survive."

She set the bottle of Hurricane back on the tray and stood. "I trust you and Dreamer, or I wouldn't be here." She reached over and gently squeezed his hand. "So what do we do first?"

# Chapter Eleven

An hour later, they had a plan on how to conquer Storm Hollow. Ginger procured a list of current Enforcers, but not much had changed while Nightmare and Dreamer had been away; most of the same Enforcers were still in charge.

After Queen Shower's demise, Queen Lisa—in the next territory—merged the two areas, but had yet to enforce her rule. Having left the area hanging in the balance, it was Kayla's duty to return the territory to its previous order.

"Do you think Shadow Mother will meet our requests?"

"It's worth a try. She has always been fair to each ruler. Our requests are not outrageous," Dreamer told her, while Nightmare remained silent.

"Nightmare?" She wanted him to tell her everything would be fine.

"Dreamer's correct. Shadow Mother *is* fair, but transferring Enforcers to another territory, especially without a council meeting, is tricky. Either way, we'll overcome this. Even if they must stay in Storm Hollow, they don't have to be your Enforcers."

Nightmare's unease about her territory weighed on her mind. She tried to brush it off but it kept nagging at her, demanding an answer. "Nightmare, you don't believe she sent us to Storm Hollow to have us killed, do you?"

"No, she has prophesied about you for too long to see you killed before you even begin. There must be another reason. Storm Hollow must play a part in the outcome or she would not have sent us there." His tone edged with confidence, making Kayla breathe easier.

Ginger stepped into the room. "Shadow Mother's waiting for you in the dining room." Message delivered, she scurried off as quick as she'd come, allowing them to make their own way to the dining room.

"Kayla, don't fret. Dreamer and I have a history in Storm Hollow, but it's a magnificent town, and you'll feel at home. Now come, let's enjoy dinner, and then we'll take you to your new home. We have much to attend to."

She took a deep breath. It was too late now that she already had both feet in this world. Next stop, Storm Hollow, a magnificent town but with powerful enemies lying in wait for her men. She tried not to think of the disasters that could be waiting for them. The thought of losing the two men she had come to trust—and adore—made her ill.

<hr>

The dining room was as long as her whole apartment and could've easily fit fifty people around the long mahogany table dominating the length of the chamber. The beautiful ivory lace table runner caught her gaze. *Where did she find one long enough for this?* The wall on the other side was made of glass and offered a view across the beautiful garden that led to a patio and swimming pool that was so long it reached around the corner of the house.

She never expected there to be such stunning architectural details. When she heard the name, she expected a dark and shadowy place. True, the sun didn't shine here, but the same could be said for Sweetwater. Not having the sun did little to detract from what she saw.

Shadow Mother sat at the head of the table, with two places set on one side of her and a third on the other. "Sit, I'm sure you have much you wish to discuss."

When Dreamer walked around the table to one place setting, she had a feeling Shadow Mother had expected her to sit there. That left the chair between the regal woman and Nightmare for Kayla. From the significant look on her face, Kayla suspected her seating choice said something.

"Thank you, Shadow Mother." He took a seat only after he held out the chair for Kayla. "If it's convenient, we wish to discuss some concerns we have about Storm Hollow."

"Ginger, please bring us a few bottles of Hurricane, and the glasses. Dinner is not a place to drink out of those bottles." Once Ginger scurried off, she turned back to Nightmare. "Proceed."

"I'm sure you're aware of the fact that we'll run into strong opposition in direct relation to what occurred there." Nightmare was interrupted by a laugh from Shadow Mother.

"What occurred there…you mean murdering Queen Shower? Seems you take it very lightly, Nightmare. Maybe my punishment should have been more severe." The threat of her torture dripped from each syllable, sending chills down Kayla's spine.

"I apologize if I gave that impression, Shadow Mother. I've never taken it lightly." Nightmare bowed his head.

The way he groveled at her feet turned Kayla's stomach. There had to be some dark, painful history—torture—between them for Nightmare to be this ill at ease around her. He was not a man she expected to see fear in but, unless she was reading him wrong, that had been the undercurrent of his actions since they arrived.

Shadow Mother waved her hand as if it didn't matter. "Proceed, Nightmare."

"There are a number of Enforcers who were strong supporters of

Queen Shower. It's likely we'll have altercations with them, especially after they are removed from their duties. We would ask they be transferred to another territory. Perhaps Queen Lisa's, since she was the one controlling Storm Hollow until now."

"You wish me to rip them from their homes…to what, make things easier for you? After all, you put yourself in this situation." Shadow Mother let out a wicked snicker.

"I'm aware of my transgression, but my concern lies with Queen Kayla. As her Enforcer in Charge, my first duty is to keep her safe at any cost."

"Enforcer in Charge? Did you make her aware that you murdered Queen Shower before she gave you that position?" She seemed incredulous, unable to believe Kayla would make such a decision—a choice she viewed as foolhardy.

"Shadow Mother, if I may speak…" She waited a prudent beat for the woman's approval, but when it didn't come, she continued. "I'm aware of the offense Nightmare committed. I'm also aware of the reason behind it. I still feel he's the best person for the position of my Enforcer in Charge. I have to trust someone in this new world, and I'm trusting Nightmare and Dreamer to keep me safe."

"That's good because you're trusting them with your life. With Nightmare as your Enforcer in Charge, you'll be painting a bull's-eye on your back. Maybe I shall rephrase that…a *bigger* bull's-eye. You already had one before you accepted them."

"Well, if I plan to survive they're my best chance. I know they'll keep me safe." Kayla wanted to reach over and lay her hand on Nightmare's, to let him know she believed him, but she needed to establish herself to everyone here, including Shadow Mother. Her actions had to show Shadow Mother that this was what she wanted. Embracing Nightmare, even just his hand, would be seen as a gesture of weakness and they couldn't afford to appear weak in front of anyone.

"That's a big risk you're taking." Shadow Mother warned as she picked up her glass.

"I was always told without risk there can be no gain." She left out the fact that it was her father's advice. She doubted bringing up her father would ease the tension in the room.

"How many Enforcers are we talking about?" Shadow Mother asked, steering them back onto the original topic.

Nightmare drew her attention. "Twelve."

"Isn't that like asking for the moon, Nightmare?" Shadow Mother set her glass down with such force the liquid sloshed out. Anger sizzled around her like a tangible aura.

"We mean no disrespect..." Kayla swallowed her apology when Shadow Mother raised her hand.

"Disrespect meant or not is still disrespect. Nightmare knows how Shadow Providence runs, any illusion he had of being able to remove *twelve* Enforcers from one territory is just that...an illusion."

"We'll be grateful for any help you can provide. We came to this meeting with the understanding that it might not be possible to remove all Enforcers. That being said, any who are identified as potential threats and remain in Storm Hollow will be removed from their duties. This will leave Enforcers without jobs, their training going to waste."

Kayla's studied the silent Dreamer while his brother spoke. Why hadn't Dreamer said anything? Were there more unwritten rules about their new positions?

"Nightmare, you bring forth a good argument and it's your right as the new Queen's Enforcer in Charge to choose the Enforcers of your territory."

Shadow Mother stared out the window, quiet for a moment. "Queen Lisa has requested to retain a number of Enforcers currently stationed in Storm Hollow. I'll grant her request and that will take care of seven of the Enforcers on your list. After dinner, go over the remaining five Enforcers and select three. Those three will then be transferred here to replace the two I have lost. The other two will remain in Storm Hollow until the next committee meeting, where they may seek a new territory."

"Thank you, Shadow Mother. It's most appreciated," Nightmare said.

Kayla wrung her hands in her lap, somewhat surprised by the outcome. What would they do with the remaining two over the coming months, and would they be a threat to her and her men? *Where are we going to get new Enforcers before the next council meeting?*

# Chapter Twelve

Kayla sat on the patio between Nightmare and Dreamer, watching the way the lights glistened off the pool water. They went over the names of the five Enforcers who remained after Queen Lisa's request. Nightmare listed the qualifications and the concerns for each Enforcer and wanted Kayla's input on which two to keep.

"Kayla, are you paying attention?" Dreamer nudged her.

She looked up, bemused. "Umm…no. I was lost in thought."

Nightmare leaned close. "We're almost done here. Let's make this last decision and proceed from there."

She nodded. Nightmare and Dreamer's demeanor changed since being in Shadow Mother's presence. Once they were in her territory, she hoped things would return to how they had been before their journey to Shadow Providence. The casual touches she enjoyed over the last few days in her apartment were gone. They either kept their hands at their sides or clasped behind them as if they were soldiers in the military. Never touching her, and when they made eye contact, it was always professional, lacking any warmth.

"You know these Enforcers, which two do you think are less dangerous to us?"

"This is supposed to be *your* decision." Nightmare pushed the paper toward her.

"What do you want me to do? Throw darts at the paper, the two it lands on are the ones we keep? How can I make an informed decision if I don't know these Enforcers?" She looked at the paper and was surprised to see a name she recognized.

It must have shown on her face because Dreamer leaned closer to her. "What is it?"

"Thunder…"

"I don't understand." Dreamer raised his eyebrow in question. "Is he one of the ones you want to keep, or send to Shadow Mother?"

She shook her head, causing a strand of her blonde hair to fall in her eyes. "Describe him," she said breathlessly. Thunder was an unusual name, making her certain it was the same man she knew.

"He's one of the older Enforcers and has been around longer than any of us. Thunder's good, but we're unsure where his loyalties are," Dreamer told her.

"His hair is like a storm cloud, a deep gray with streaks of light and dark mixed in."

"You just described Thunder as if you saw him before. But how could that be possible?" Nightmare's squinted as he watched her curiously.

She looked around the courtyard to make sure no one was near before she leaned in and whispered. "He came to my world…to visit when I was a child."

"You mean…"

"Yes. He seemed to be a friend. I was young, but I remember those *visits*." She put extra emphasis on visits trying to make it clear to Nightmare and Dreamer that Thunder had come to visit her father on more than one occasion.

Dreamer spoke up, after a few moments of letting it all sink in. "I'm not sure if we should trust him or not."

"It's questionable, but I think he might be a risk we should take. He'll be a great asset to us if it turns out his loyalties do not lie with Queen Shower. Either way it will give us time to get our questions answered." Nightmare looked back at the paper in front of her and pointed to a name. "Chameleon is the other I believe we should keep. His ability to disappear in plain sight will be useful to us. It's also something that would give another Queen power to use against us if we turned him over."

"Then let's inform Shadow Mother and go."

As if expecting them to be finished, Shadow Mother strolled onto the patio. "Have you made your decision?" she asked, coming to stand before them.

"Yes. We would like…"

Shadow Mother stopped her before she could continue. "I have called the Enforcers and they're waiting in the dining hall. We'll inform them of the decisions. The two you have chosen will return with you this night, the rest will go on their way."

Shadow Mother turned on her heel and headed back inside, leaving them no choice but to follow her. Kayla lagged a little. The unease in her men, Shadow Mother's manner, and the utterly surreal sensation of being in another world left her with the feeling that she was the lamb and this was her trip to the slaughter. The Enforcers waiting in the dining hall were prejudiced against her men, and it was possible these people she'd never met were about to lose their homes.

*Because of me.*

# Chapter Thirteen

Kayla felt out of place under the watchful, assessing gazes of so many strangers. The men lined the far side of table. She recognized Thunder the moment she saw him, and from his reaction, she gathered he recognized her as well. He cut his gaze away from her as soon as their eyes met.

"Enforcers, thank you for coming. This is Queen Kayla, the new ruler of Storm Hollow. We have gathered you here because some of you will be assigned new territories. Queen Lisa has requested seven of you. As I call your name, exit to meet Rod, Queen Lisa's Enforcer in Charge. He will lead you to your new territory. Your belongings will be sent to you this evening."

While Shadow Mother read the list of names, Kayla's mind wandered back to Thunder. He returned many times to visit her father; if he meant them harm he would've done it already. At least that's what she tried to convince herself of. Her father's reaction to Nightmare and Dreamer still played out in her mind. *Does he think we're here to kill him? Or is he here to kill me?*

So many questions. Her father should have been the one to answer them—to tell her of this place and their part in it. She wondered if Thunder would be willing to do so, or if he would only make her more confused.

As the last Enforcer filed out of the room, she focused on the scene playing out in front of her in time for Shadow Mother to turn the floor over to her. "Queen Kayla has decided that two other Enforcers will return to

Storm Hollow with her. The other three will remain here to replace Nightmare and Dreamer." Shadow Mother turned to her. "Please inform them of your decision."

She cleared her throat, her heart pounding, her skin clammy, then forced the words out. "Chameleon and Thunder, you'll return to Storm Hollow with us. This is in no way assurance that you will remain as Enforcers. That decision will be made when I have spoken with you. I will not trust my life or the life of the Stormkins in my territory to you unless I'm convinced you're the right ones for the job." She watched the Enforcers for any sign of relief or irritation over her decision, but neither showed the faintest reaction.

Were these men so cold they just didn't care, or were they trying to hide the fact they wanted to be part of her demise? Maybe they feared retribution under Shadow Mother's watchful eye.

"Very well. As for the remaining three, Ginger will show you to your quarters. Your training will begin at daybreak." With that, Shadow Mother left them.

"My Queen, we should make our way to your territory." Nightmare told her when they were alone. "There are cars waiting for us out front. The bags are already loaded."

"Cars?" She asked unable to believe they wouldn't be using one of those portals again.

"We have vehicles. They are normally only used for short travels to save time. But if you prefer, we could use the portal."

She balked, thinking of the discomfort caused by that mode of transportation. "No thank you. A car is much preferred to another trip through the portal so soon."

On her way back down the entryway hall, she took a final look around, wondering what she would find when she reached Storm Hollow. Not the type for big formal houses, she wanted something that would feel like home, something cozy and modest. A place for her and her men to be at ease.

Outside she found two large black SUVs. "Thunder, Chameleon, take the second SUV and follow us," Nightmare ordered as he tossed the keys to Dreamer, and directed her to the backseat of the SUV. He slid in next to her and pressed his finger to her lips to ensure her silence. With a nod, Dreamer started the engine.

She raised her eyebrow in question. He slid his hand into his pocket and pulled out a small black stone. Cradling it in his palm, he blew a hot breath across it until it glowed a soft blue.

"It's a privacy shield," Nightmare explained as he placed it on the armrest between the driver and passenger seats. "It encircles the car ensuring no one can listen to what we say."

"We should be worried about people eavesdropping while we're driving?"

"As Queen you should always be concerned about eavesdroppers. There was nothing we could do at Shadow Mother's. We were in her home, it's her right to listen if she desires, but in the car and your land we will take precautions. There could be bugs planted in your territory to spy on you because not everybody will support or believe the prophecies about you. Other Queens will also take offense to you accepting half-breeds and cast-outs in your territory, making you more of a target. Once we have dealt with Thunder and Chameleon, we will secure the house," Nightmare said. "You'll have similar devises placed throughout your quarters and other key areas of the house to ensure you are not overheard."

"I didn't know I had to worry about that. I suspected not everybody here would accept me, but I didn't realize it would be this bad...with listening devices and everything." She stared out the window, considering the fate that had befallen her. *Is Dad right?*

"Kayla, Dreamer and I will protect you with our lives. We won't let anything happen to you. Trust us." He laid his hand on her thigh, but what she wanted was to be wrapped in his arms. She wanted to feel his warm embrace against her skin, reassuring her.

Outside the window, it didn't look much different from her world, yet she knew it was. Would she ever really be a part of this strange new place she was now supposed to live in? Or would being here cost her more than she wanted to give up? Mainly the two men who sat with her now.

"You and Dreamer are different in Shadow Mother's presence. Why? What does she hold over you?" She caught Dreamer glancing in the rearview mirror, but when their eyes met he turned his attention back to the road. When the silence continued, she demanded an answer.

"Shadow Mother is the ruler of all Stormkins. She tends to use Enforcers as examples to other Stormkins," Nightmare replied, sinking against the back of the seat.

"You fear her." It was a statement with deep impact on everyone in the SUV.

"She's only fair until you get on her bad side, unless you're a Queen or a royal consort. I've been on the receiving end of her punishments—her tortures—more times than I care to recount. I'm respectful of her because I know what she's capable of." Nightmare was unable to meet her gaze.

She rested her hand over his. "I'm sorry. She had no right…"

"She has every right. She's the supreme ruler of this land."

"Nightmare, that gives her no right to torture you or anyone else."

"You have a good heart, but no matter the prophecies, if you go up against her she'll kill us all." He squeezed her hand.

"What are these prophecies you keep mentioning?" She changed the subject, but she wouldn't let it go for long. She could not stand idly by if Shadow Mother was torturing people. She'd be left with no choice but to step in if Shadow Mother tried to harm Nightmare, Dreamer, or any of the people in her territory. She wouldn't stand by and let the men she had grown to care about or anyone she was supposed to protect fall under Shadow Mother's punishment.

"I told you before, you'll be a safe haven to half-breeds and the unwanted." As Nightmare spoke, Dreamer turned on a back road leading out of town.

"You say prophecies like there's more than one."

"Tell her. Keeping her in the dark won't help. Storm Hollow is already an uphill battle. She needs to know everything." It was the first time Dreamer spoke since they left Shadow Mother, and Kayla was grateful to have him on her side.

"In short...you're the key to defeating the Sunkins," Nightmare said.

"The what?" She wanted to make sure she heard correctly.

"The key. Without you we can't defeat them. They're growing stronger and more dangerous to humans with each day. You'll help us stop them. I'm not sure how yet, but it will happen. What other Queens don't realize is that strong Enforcers and warriors are the backbone to keeping them safe. They see the Enforcer's power as a threat to their authority and that will be their downfall. It will also be the reason why you succeed. Those Enforcers and warriors are the ones we need to bring into our ranks."

"Why me?"

"I don't know the answer to that, but I'm sure the question will be answered soon. In the meantime, we need to discuss Thunder. Did you notice he wouldn't make eye contact with you? I believe he recognized you."

"You caught that, did you? I haven't seen him in years."

"You look as though you remember something. What is it?"

"The last time I saw him…I had just entered high school. Dad and I were having an argument when he came…my anger had control of me."

Nightmare waited for her to finish, while Dreamer's gaze flicked between the road before them and her. Dreamer prompted her. "What happened?"

"The house was like a tornado, papers flying all over the downstairs. When he strolled into the house, something snapped inside of me and every window in the house broke—picture frames, glasses, everything. I crumpled to the floor, my energy drained."

"You have telekinesis." Admiration colored Dreamer's voice.

"*Tella* what?

"Telekinesis. It means you can move something with your mind. It's a rare ability among our kind." Dreamer smiled at her via the rearview mirror.

"I think you got the wrong idea, I can't move anything."

"We'll have to test this out later, but look, we're entering your territory." Dreamer nodded toward the windows.

As she watched they came into a group of lights; she was keenly aware of Nightmare's silence beside her. *What did I say that was wrong?*

"This is the Main Street of Storm Hollow. There are a few businesses along here that generate part of your income. We'll discuss those later, but look straight ahead. Do you see those lights on top of the hill?" Dreamer didn't wait for her to answer. "It's the main house, your house. The Enforcers' barracks and cottages for some of the elite Enforcers are around the other side, closer to the road."

"It's huge." She was stunned.

"Queens go all out with their houses. There are twelve bedroom suites. Numerous guest bedrooms, sitting rooms, as well as a library, media room, and indoor pool. In your world you would consider it a mansion."

"I don't need all that. Who else will live there with me?" Her mouth hung slightly agape.

"For each Queen, that's different. Some choose to have selected live-in Enforcers, whereas others, such as Shadow Mother, allows no one other than staff in the house. There's normally a chef, and storm elf—like Keenan—who are live-in staff." As Dreamer spoke he turned onto another road that lead up a steep incline, leading to the house.

"What about you and Nightmare?" She didn't want to be separated from the two men she trusted most.

"You can decide. Thunder and Chameleon should be the only ones in residence in the Enforcers' quarters. We can either stay there or one of the cottages. Most Queens would either give Nightmare one of the cottages, or have him kept close at hand in the main house, since he's the Enforcer in Charge. But it's your decision where to place any of us."

"Very well." She looked around as the house came into view. A gate with a gatekeeper came into view, making her smile. "I didn't know anyone even had gatekeepers anymore."

Dreamer flashed the badge Shadow Mother had handed her earlier that day. It marked Dreamer as one of her elite Enforcers and she had others to hand out to whomever else they chose. Nightmare had his own; it was slightly different to show his status as her Enforcer in Charge. Without a badge, no one would be allowed onto the grounds or near her without the Enforcer in Charge's approval. She looked at Nightmare, who remained silent next to her. "What's wrong?"

"It's nothing you've done. I'm considering everything we need to do tonight." He turned his attention away from her and focused on Dreamer. "Dreamer, Kayla, and I will meet with Thunder, then Chameleon. I want you to meet with the storm elf and chef, find out if they can be trusted. Then have the storm elf gather the other Enforcers' belongings to send to them. Ours are in the back with Kayla's, we'll deal with them later."

Dreamer pulled the SUV to a stop in front of the main house and nodded to his brother. He shut off the engine, but Kayla stopped him before he could get out.

"Wait." With their gazes on her, she gathered her courage. "I want you both in the main house near me. Unless—" She glanced nervously toward the floor as she swallowed the lump that was slowly forming in her throat. "You don't want to be…or…it would be seen as a weakness."

For the first time since coming to Shadow Providence, her men smiled at her. Nightmare pushed her hair out of her face, the gesture endearing and gentle. "There's nowhere else we would rather be."

She released a breath she'd been holding, nodded, and climbed out of the vehicle.

# Chapter Fourteen

The house even possessed a conference room that reminded her of something one might find in a luxury hotel. The walls were painted a cool shade of gray. A long mahogany table surrounded by black leather chairs dominated the room and expensive paintings decorated the walls adding color to the very business-like atmosphere.

She sat with Nightmare, staring across the table at Thunder. She wanted to speak with Thunder first, hoping he might provide her with the answers her father hadn't. She believed in coming straight to the point. No use in dragging the session out any longer than it had to be.

"You recognize me, don't you?"

"Queen, you must have me confused with someone else." He refused to meet her gaze, staring down at the table.

"No, I don't believe I have. I know you as well as you know me, now let's dropped this bullshit and get to the point."

"Thunder, if you're concerned about someone overhearing you, don't be." Nightmare leaned forward, his clasped hands resting on the table. "I have already searched the room for bugs and it's clean. Tell us why you were visiting her father and it will go no further than this room. Draw this out and I'll be sure to inform Shadow Mother of your treason."

The mention of Shadow Mother scared Thunder enough to talk.

"Nighthawk's a dear friend. Even after his betrayal of our people, I visited when I was in the area."

His sudden willingness to cooperate had Kayla wondering if Thunder had been on the receiving end of Shadow Mother's torture.

"You risked her wrath to see a friend." There was a heavy dose of surprise in Nightmare's voice.

"I did. He's more like a brother to me than a friend. I tried to get him to go to Shadow Mother instead of leaving like he did, but he wouldn't."

"Why?" More than anything else, Kayla needed to know the answer to that.

"You should ask him."

"I have and instead of giving me the answers…" She waved it off, not wanting to get into what happened the last time she saw her father. "Let's just say he had no interest in telling me."

"I'm sure it was a shock to see you with him." Thunder nodded his head toward Nightmare.

"Why, because my father was the reason Illusion was killed?" Kayla leaned forward, anger surfacing. Thunder believed her father had done nothing wrong.

"Illusion's death isn't his fault. There was a battle going on."

"A battle my father left in the middle of, leaving Illusion, Dreamer, and countless others without his backup." She pushed away from the table, fury clawing at her skin. "If it had been your brother wouldn't you have felt as though it was at least partially his fault? You're lying if you tell me no."

"He chose the wrong time to leave, but everyone makes mistakes. To exile him from our land because of it wasn't justified." Thunder watched her intently.

"You believe that don't you?" She didn't give him time to answer because she already knew his answer. "My father or not, I think he got off easy."

She let out a heartfelt laugh, as her father's words replayed in her mind, with all the values he drilled into her growing up. "I was taught the punishment should fit the crime. An eye for an eye. You know who taught me that? My father. The same man who abandoned his people in battle, leaving at least one dead and another scarred for life."

Thunder looked up at her, anger in his eyes. "Are you saying…"

"That my father should have been *killed* for his crime? Yes, that's exactly what I'm saying. The punishment should fit the crime and justice should be sought for the victims. What justice did Nightmare and Dreamer have?" Her emotions seemed to have more control over her than she would have preferred. Her gaze fell on Nightmare before she continued. "The values he instilled in me run deep and true. I can't overlook what he did just because he's my father. His actions cost at least one life."

"You would condemn your own father to die?" Thunder asked, shock lacing his voice. "He's your father."

"I know who he is. He's the one who raised me, but he's also the one who drilled these values into me. If he can't live by them, how could he expect me to? Regardless of how I feel, what happens to him isn't up to me. Shadow Mother has already made that decision. His return would be equivalent to signing his own death warrant." She leaned against the chair she'd vacated. Nightmare still sat across from Thunder staring at him and it seemed as though the tension rose with each passing second.

"You're more like your father than either of us would have guessed." Thunder's lips curled into a small smile. "Your father would be proud. You'll make an excellent Queen."

"I'm sure Queen Kayla has more questions, but we need the most important one answered now," Nightmare said firmly. "You risked everything to visit Nighthawk but I don't believe it was just for friendship. You know something—something he hasn't even told his daughter. Where do your loyalties lie? With Queen Shower? Nighthawk? Shadow Mother?"

"What I know isn't for me to say." He looked from Nightmare to Kayla again, and Kayla caught a faint trace of sympathy in his eyes. "My loyalties are not with the former ruler. I, like you, have been at the receiving end of her tortures. I was glad to see her go. Shadow Mother is the supreme ruler of this land. But as an Enforcer, my loyalties are *supposed* to remain with the Queen I serve."

His words tasted like the truth to Kayla, but she caught the underlying tone. "Supposed to? That doesn't answer the question." She was starting to feel as if they were going around in circles when it came to Nighthawk, and she could barely believe he was the same man who raised her. She wasn't sure if they would ever get a direct answer out of Thunder.

"I have more years behind me then I care to recount; therefore, I'm more outspoken than other Enforcers. So be it if a ruler, or even Shadow Mother, wishes my death because of it. I've grown tired of the games and I'll only give my complete devotion if a Queen deserves it. Nighthawk has been like family, but the only loyalty I have where he's concerned is that I wouldn't kill him, no matter who ordered his death. I've never given him Stormkin information, or even spoke of our world. I'd visit to check in on you two, bring him a bottle or two of Hurricane; he always said there was nothing Earthside like a good bottle of Hurricane."

She pulled out the chair, took a seat again, and leaned forward. "A Queen shouldn't have to earn your loyalties. She should have it from the moment she steps into power, like a sheriff taking over a new police department. You only have the power a Queen gives you." She turned her attention to Nightmare. "Unless he's going to give us some straight answers, he can find a new territory to serve."

She reached for the bottle of water sitting in the middle of the table while the men stared each other down. *What is this, some kind of pissing contest?*

"Queen Kayla, you don't understand our world, our Queens…or how cruel they can be. Even being raised with humans, you still strongly believe your father should die for his actions." Thunder leaned back in his chair, his focus completely on her.

"Thunder, I'll be a Queen unlike any other. I'll be fair and kind, but I won't tolerate anyone who disregards the rules. Treason and abandonment will be punished to the fullest extent. I'll protect my Enforcers. No one—not Shadow Mother, not another Queen—will touch my people. I don't believe in torture and I won't stand for it when it comes to my people. If one of my Enforcers has done something then I'll deal with them and the punishment will fit the crime." She was irritated with Thunder and wanted answers from him. She wanted him dealt with if he was a threat. His doubt was almost overwhelming.

Why not leave if he hated the world he lived in, or at least step down from his position as an Enforcer? She made a mental note to ask Nightmare about it later. Maybe he could give some insight as to what happened to Enforcers when they left their positions, or maybe they never left.

"You can't protect your Enforcers. Enforcers are there to protect the Queen, not the other way around," Thunder said gruffly.

"Not here. Here I'll make sure no one suffers the tortures others have inflicted upon them in the past. My men will be safe and in return, I only ask for their loyalty and trust." She relaxed in her chair. "That will be all for now. Think of where your loyalties are. Until we know for sure, you're removed of all of your duties, and not permitted to leave the grounds. You may stay in the Enforcers' barracks for the time being. We'll expect an answer within twenty-four hours. Pledge your allegiance to me as your Queen or request permission to seek another ruler at the next council meeting."

He pushed back from his chair and rose. "I don't know if I should be pleased or disappointed in how your father raised you. You have the potential to be a good Queen, but you could be taken down before you even begin if you continue to trust the men you have surrounded yourself with." He left without another word.

When the door shut securely behind him, she stretched her legs, and walked to the window. The conference room sat on the backside of the house, giving a view down the mountain and overlooking the town—her territory. The hour grew late, lights flickered off, and yet they still had much to do.

"My Queen, we should deal with Chameleon."

She turned to find that Nightmare had slightly angled his chair so he could look at her. She frowned, crossing her arms over her chest. "There seems to be such hostility in Thunder, but I can't figure out if it's for me or for you. Do you have history with him?"

"Thunder and I have come across each other in the past, but never enough to cause the hatred he has. I believe it might stem more from your beliefs and willingness to see punishment brought down on Nighthawk. He seems to know more than he's telling us…the way he said you need to speak to Nighthawk leads me to believe this."

Alone with Nightmare, she wanted to feel his touch, but he sat there. His expression was unreadable and once again she noted the key difference between Nightmare and Dreamer. They looked so much alike but their personalities were polar opposites. Nightmare was hard to read, formal, and reserved; she might even go as far to say that he was uptight. While Dreamer had been quieter with Shadow Mother, he was more relaxed and open when he was with Kayla. Her men seemed to balance each other out.

"What do you think is the best way to find out what he knows?"

"Your father." Nightmare shrugged.

"You can't be serious. You think he'll tell me anything after our last encounter with him?"

He rose and strolled to the window to stand next to her. Reaching her, he placed his hand on the small of her back, standing slightly behind her as they looked out the window together. He was quiet for a long moment. "There are ways to get the truth from someone."

She turned to face him. "What do you mean?"

"The simplest is your power of touch. Touch him and find the answer you seek. Another is Dreamer's ability to enter another's dreams. He could enter Nighthawk's dreams and find the answer for you." He drew her closer, then raised his arm and brought his other hand up to lay it on her forearm, gently rubbing up and down. "Or you could try to call him. Maybe he'll answer your questions now that he's had time to think things through."

*Will dad give me the answers I need?* She didn't know, but she would figure out a way to get to the bottom of it, that much was certain.

# Chapter Fifteen

"Have a seat, Chameleon," Kayla said when he entered the room. "We just need to go over a few things to see if you're a suitable Enforcer. If not, you can seek permission to search for a new position at the next council meeting."

"My Queen, if I may…" Chameleon lowered his long body into the chair across from them and waited for her nod before he continued. "I was promoted to Enforcer after Queen Lisa took over the territory. I wasn't here under Queen Shower, the one Nightmare…"

She made a mental note that he referred to her as *My Queen*. The address showed respect and acceptance.

"Killed?" she questioned. "I'm aware of what happened and that doesn't change the here and now. Honestly, I don't care if you were an Enforcer under her or the pool boy. What I care about is whether or not you'll be loyal to me."

"Yes, I will be. If I could explain why, it might assist in relieving any apprehensions you might have about my service." He paused for a moment and took a sip from the bottle of water in front of him. "I'm a half-breed. My father was a Stormkin and he fell in love while on a mission in your world. My mother—a human—died in childbirth. He returned here with me and that's when my father's disloyalty came out. Queen Shower killed him. My uncle took me in and raised me, but I've always been an outcast. I was only promoted because my ability became known."

"Disloyal for sleeping with a human?" she inquired, unsure if there was something else Chameleon didn't mention.

When Chameleon stumbled on the question, his lip quivering as he tried to find the words, Nightmare raised a hand and took over. "In our land, Enforcers are celibate unless they're sleeping with their Queen. Enforcers might be fertile and their only responsibility is to their ruler. Allowing them to…fornicate with other women could divide their loyalties, especially if they'd married."

"Oh…" She couldn't believe the men stood for this practice. They could spend decades—centuries—without the touch of woman. She filed it away for future consideration.

"Chameleon, your ability is pretty special from what I gather. However, it means nothing to me if I can't trust you. I would rather have you out of my territory if you present a danger to me."

"Queen Kayla is different than any other you've encountered," Nightmare interjected. "She requires loyalty more than anything else. She'll be on your side if you pledge your allegiance to her. She doesn't care about half-breed status, everyone has a place in her territory."

Chameleon appeared relieved. "My Queen, I have heard the prophecies about you and it would be an honor to serve you. My loyalties would be to you and only you."

Nightmare nodded and stood. "Chameleon, if you could wait in the hall and give us a moment, we'll have an answer for you shortly. There's something we need to deal with first and it will give you time to make sure this is the right decision for you."

Chameleon didn't question or even look Kayla's way as he rose and strolled out of the room. He seemed to respect that Nightmare was her Enforcer in Charge and that he was an extension of her. When Nightmare gave an order, it was as if she gave the command, and it had to be obeyed in the same fashion.

"I can taste the truth in his words," she told Nightmare when the door closed behind Chameleon.

"There's one way to know for sure." He laid his hand on top of hers. "Touch him and you'll know. But I believe him. If he's willing to pledge his allegiance to you, then I believe it would be wise to retain his services as an Enforcer."

Nightmare's cell phone vibrated where it sat on the table. He glanced at the display. "Dreamer," he told her before answering.

While Nightmare spoke to Dreamer, she pulled her own cell phone out of her pocket and debated whether she wanted to call her father. She didn't like being in this new world without knowing the secret her father was hiding from her.

She unlocked the phone and ran her finger through her contacts. Nightmare hung up before she could decide to place the call.

"Dreamer has spoken with the storm elf and chef. They're cleared and wish to remain in your service. We need to finish this because there's something else that requires your attention."

"What is it?"

"Let's deal with Chameleon first." He walked to the door with determination and she couldn't help but admire the way his butt looked in his dress slacks. He'd slipped out of his suit jacket sometime after their arrival, but he still looked like the CEO of a major corporation, not her Enforcer in Charge. She wanted to cup her hand over his butt cheek and give it a squeeze.

With Chameleon's oath-taking, she had three Enforcers. Nightmare led her to her personal suite where Dreamer waited and on the way he discussed her need for increased protection. They would have to interview potential Enforcers. He made it clear he wanted a core group of trusted men before the next council meeting.

"How are we supposed to find Enforcers when they've all been sent away?" She took another step before she realized he'd stopped walking. She turned around to stare back at him. "What? It was a simple question."

He took a step to close the gap between them and raised his hand. He slid a strand of hair away from her face and she pressed her cheek into his palm. The warmth of his touch made her cheeks heat; he ran his thumb over her lips as if he was wondering how she would taste. She forgot all about the dangers that surrounded her and just wanted to kiss him—to feel his lips against hers.

"There are very few I would trust with your life, but there's one Stormkin I'd like you to meet tomorrow. I believe he would make an excellent Enforcer." He leaned down and for brief moment she thought he would finally kiss her. Instead, he placed a timid peck on her cheek. "Come, my Queen, Dreamer's waiting."

Disappointment flooded through her body. *Why didn't he kiss me? Could it be because I'm not a true Stormkin, or because he is my Enforcer in Charge?* As they reached the end of the hallway, she ran out of time to question it further.

"This is your bedroom suite," Nightmare explained as he wrapped his hand around the door handle. "Dreamer and I have taken one on either side of you. The staff lives on the first floor at the other end near the kitchen. There should be no one else in this area but the three of us. Dreamer has already swept the rooms for bugs and has installed the same devices we used in the car. There should be no problems now."

She nodded, slipped into the room and immediately searched for Dreamer. She found the suit jacket he had worn to meet Shadow Mother; he'd tossed casually at the end of her bed. The man stood at the window, his arms crossed over his toned chest, his hair tie pulled loose. A worried expression creased his face.

She walked to him, closing the space between them quickly. "Dreamer, what is it?"

"I brought our belongings up…"

"If something isn't there or damaged it can be replaced." She glanced at his brother for some help, but Nightmare only stepped to the bed to examine the open suitcase.

"I wasn't going through your stuff, my Queen. When I sat it down, it sprang open."

"You didn't do it, Dreamer." Nightmare turned from the suitcase back to them, holding out an envelope. "It seems as if Shadow Mother has more instructions for us."

"I saw it lying there when it popped open and that's when I called you."

Kayla gave Dreamer's arm a reassuring squeeze. "We'll deal with whatever it is." Her men, who feared nothing, feared Shadow Mother and her wrath. But she vowed nothing would happen to them while she was in charge.

Nightmare held out the envelope. "Open it."

She sat on the bed and slit the envelope open. Her heart beat frantically against her chest. Inside she found a piece of heavy stationary.

*The ring on your finger from your father is one that has been passed down through Stormkin families for centuries. The ring has the ability to find fertile pairs with a simple touch. I have loaned you two of my best Enforcers. In order to keep the brothers, the ring must prove you could be a fertile match with both of them. If the ring chooses one or both of them you have twenty-four hours to bed them. Once the twenty-four hours have passed if they haven't been in your bed, they must return to me.*

*Our numbers have been dwindling for many years. You'll restore fertility with the birth of your child. The prophecy says you'll bring much change to the Stormkins before you give birth. You have five years from this day to make your changes and produce a child. Otherwise you'll lose your crown and be exiled from Shadow Providence.*

*The twenty-four hours began when you left my house.*

The note fell out of her hand and the world seemed to swallow her. The rabbit hole she fell through earlier seemed to have a second drop. She couldn't believe Shadow Mother was not only ordering her to sleep with Nightmare and Dreamer, but also to have a child. How could she bring a child into a world she'd only just entered? Things were too unstable to add an innocent infant into the equation, but she'd lose her men if she refused.

# Chapter Sixteen

"Kayla, look at me." Nightmare placed his hands on her shoulders and gently shook her. It was enough to lift the fog that surrounded her since opening the envelope. "I know this is a shock for you and we'll support whatever decision you make."

While she remained frozen in shock, her men read the letter and awaited her decision.

"Whatever decision I make…" she stammered, "you…you make it sound as if I have one. I won't let Shadow Mother take you two from me. Where does she get the nerve…can she even do this?"

"I'm afraid she can as supreme ruler of our land. Once you have established your territory, she won't be able to order Enforcers away unless it is for punishment for a crime committed outside of your territory." Nightmare removed his hands from her shoulders, but remained close enough to touch.

"Does that mean…" Dreamer spoke softly as he stood next to the window.

Dreamer—the more sensitive of the two—stood there holding the letter, as if his fate was sealed. She wanted to go to him and wrap her arms around him, but she wasn't sure her legs could support her.

"Yes, it does. I don't like how she's forced my hand, but…we'll do as

Shadow Mother asked. I won't let you back into her hands. But I've touched you both and the ring did nothing, does that mean…"

Nightmare cut her off before she could voice her fears. "You already experienced it." When she continued to stare at him, he continued. "The electricity you felt in our touch at your apartment. That was the earlier sign. Now that you're back in our land, you should experience a warm feeling through your hand when you touch bare skin. Touch me." He put his hand out to her, waiting for her to grasp it.

*What if nothing happens? I'll lose him.* She tried to push the thoughts aside, but the knot in her stomach wouldn't go away. She took a deep breath and then placed her hand in his. As the ring made contact with his hand a warm sensation traveled from her ring finger up the palm of her hand. Her lips curled up into a smile and she wrapped her arms around him, drawing her body close to his in excitement. She let her head rest against him a moment before turning her attention to Dreamer.

Content where she was, she held out her hand. "Come, Dreamer. Let's find out." He came to her without hesitation, placing his hand in hers. The same warm sensation spread through her again.

She forced herself away from Nightmare's warm embrace and went to Dreamer. She raised one hand to gently rub his cheek before standing on her tippy toes to kiss him. When their lips met, Dreamer slipped his arm around her waist and pulled her against him.

"Shadow Mother's curveballs won't divide us. I want to shower and then we can deal with this." She stepped out of Dreamer's grip and walked away from her men to the shower with a little hesitation. *This is the chance I've been waiting for. Nightmare might not have kissed me before but I'll feel his lips on me soon. Dreamer…two men…*

With Kayla gone, Nightmare filled Dreamer in on their meeting with Thunder and Chameleon. It gave him something to keep his mind off the fact that water was cascading down her naked body at that very moment. She was alone in the shower, and all he wanted to do was go to her and give his assistance and scrub her back. At least to start things out. Naughty visions of her wet body played out in his mind.

"She's taking this better than I expected."

"She's a strong woman. She'll make an excellent Queen. However, we need to make this a suitable territory for her to rule and a safe haven for half-breeds. We'll need to help her establish guidelines for Storm Hollow. I have some issues to see to, stay with her until I return." He stalked to the door but turned back before opening it. "Don't forget Shadow Mother's orders."

It took everything in him to shut the door behind him. He and Dreamer had always been close—close enough he didn't mind sharing a woman with him, but he wouldn't share the bed with them. His time with her would just be between them.

She emerged from the bathroom with just a towel wrapped around her to find Dreamer sitting in the small sitting area of the bedroom. The gas fireplace was on, creating a cozy, romantic atmosphere as the light from the flames danced off the walls. There was just enough light coming through the window and from the fireplace to see Dreamer.

"Nightmare…"

"I'm not worried about him." She smiled as she wandered toward him. "Right now it's only about us." She reached for the first button of his dress shirt, but he caught her hand before she could make contact.

"You don't have to do this. I can return to Shadow Mother. You need Nightmare, he'll protect you. I see the way you look at him."

"Are you saying I have to choose? Because I don't want to choose. Maybe it's selfish, but I want you both. You see how I look at him, but I look at you the same way…you just don't see it." She wiggled her hand free from his and laid it on his chest. "I won't give either of you up without a fight. Shadow Mother might have put a time limit on this, but left to our own devices, we would've done it anyway. I want you."

He turned away from her, looking back to the fire. "That will change when I take off my shirt."

"Your scars won't take away my desire for you. Let me prove it to you." She reached for the button again, and this time he didn't stop her.

"I can't bear to see a disgusted look in your eyes," he told her, unable to meet her gaze.

"Trust me," she whispered. She pulled the shirt out of his slacks as she undid the last button. He sucked in a deep breath as if bracing himself for her repulsion. Butterflies danced in her stomach, not for fear of what she would find, but for the excitement of what was coming. Tonight she would claim her men, and no one—not even Shadow Mother—could take them away from her.

She slid his shirt open, pushed it down his arms and let it fall to the floor behind. The few scars that ran down the side of his neck were nothing compared to what she found. What she thought had been done with claws or a knife, she realized were burns. It started just shy of his shoulder where the skin was deformed, hard, textured, and crawled up his neck, then down through the lower part of his chest to his arm. She ran her hand over his chest, exploring the contours of each horrible wound.

"Dreamer, look at me. Do you see disgust in my face?"

He obeyed, but said nothing.

"These change nothing. They don't lessen my desire for you. Don't give them power over you." She leaned up, bringing their lips together, and kissed him.

Longing quickly overpowered the sweet kiss she intended as he circled her waist with his arms, and drew her close. Breaking the kiss, she drew him toward the bed as eagerness thrummed through her. "Lay on the bed."

He slipped out of his shoes and socks before climbing onto the middle of the mattress. She followed and slid on top of him, straddling his waist. She wanted him naked beneath her, but first she had to remove the look of apprehension in his eyes.

Stroking his chest, she toyed with his chest hair. She wanted to open his belt and rip his pants off, but first. "Tell me how it happened."

"In battle…" His throat convulsed with a swallow, but she continued petting him and some of the tension eased in him. "It's from a fireball. Some Sunkins have the ability to throw fireballs. Normally, when a Stormkin is hit with a fireball it will kill us. It's one of the few ways to truly kill us."

"Not that I'm not thankful you're still here, but why didn't it?"

"Illusion…he stepped into the line of fire to save me. When we die, we turn to dust, what was left of the fireball passed through him and hit my shoulder. Since it wasn't a direct hit I was left scarred. If not for my brother…I'd be dead."

"If it wasn't for my father it never would've happened." She felt the scars added a layer to him, but sadness coursed through her at the thought of the damage inflicted by her father's abandonment.

"No one knows what might have happened, even with him there." He trailed a caress up her arm.

"How can you say that? Don't you blame him at least a little?"

"When it first happened, yes. I was too weak to travel—healing takes a lot out of the body—but I wanted to travel to your world and see your father

101

suffer for the damage he did. I have let it go now that time has passed. Being cast from your homeland has to be punishment enough." He rose to his elbows so he'd be close enough to kiss her lips. When their lips broke apart he added, "Now that I'm falling in love with his daughter all hatred is gone. If he didn't leave our land that day, you might never have come into my life, and that's one thing I'm not willing to give up."

She leaned down and kissed him. His lips were warm against hers and he tugged the towel free. It fell to her waist as he broke the kiss, then tumbled her onto her back. He quickly rolled on top of her before she had time to realize what had happened.

"Hey, what do you think you're doing?" she demanded playfully, her lips curling into a smile.

"You had your time, now it's my turn to explore." He kissed her neck, nibbling down her jawline to her shoulder. She unbuckled his belt and slid it out of the loops. It landed on the floor with a thump. She moaned in ecstasy when his tongue flicked over her hardened nipple; her nipples had always been extra sensitive, the slightest touch bringing her pleasure.

She tugged on his dress slacks before he could move lower. "If I'm going to be naked, these need to go." She unbuttoned them, but couldn't get them off with him on top of her.

"As my Queen wishes." He jumped off the bed and stripped off his pants. Her heart skipped a beat as he stood naked before her. She wanted to run her hands over his body, feel the tight muscles beneath his skin.

She winced when he said *my Queen*. "I'm not your Queen in bed. Anything I ask in the bedroom is just that—a favor—not an order. I don't want you to be in my bed because of my power. I want you here next to me because you want to be, not because of some loyalty."

"I apologize, I meant no disrespect."

"Dreamer," she interrupted. "Think of me as your lover…nothing else."

"You'll always be my Queen, but I want to be here with you for good. I'm not here because of some duty but because I want to be. As you said, Shadow Mother's demands only sped up what would have happened anyway. We've already felt this longing, the need to touch." He slid back onto the bed, placing his hand over hers. "It's been many years since I've been asked to share a bed with anyone. Most can barely stand looking at the scars they see, let alone the ones beneath my shirt. Don't send me away for my inability to think of you only as a lover…but also as my Queen."

"I'm not going to send you away, even if we weren't lovers. You'll always have a place in Storm Hollow, or wherever I am." She knew Queen Shower was harsh, and both of her men had been punished senselessly. She could see it in their actions and their cautiousness. Somehow, she had to prove to them she wasn't like the other Queens. She wouldn't abuse them or send them away. "Now lay back and let me put your worries to rest."

When he did as she asked she straddled his hips and wrapped her hand around his shaft. Gliding caresses up and down the hard length, she teased his erection harder. He groaned and reached up to caress her breasts. Heat coiled between her thighs and her sex clenched.

Desperate, she shifted her position and angled the head of his shaft to her core and sank down. He filled her slowly, inch by inch, and his low moan echoed hers. He pinched her nipple, the pain mingling with pleasure and she rocked upward and then down again, finding her rhythm. Impatience coiled through her and he grasped her hips, increasing his pace and driving into her with force.

The erotic dance amped up her tension, every delicious glide of his shaft inside her seemed to set off another cascade of heat. Sweat glided over her skin as he sat up, holding onto her, and her nipples rubbed against his chest—the scars adding a fresh layer of pleasure. He thrust into her faster and faster and the world shimmered. Her pleasure unfurled and she threw her head back, crying out. He pumped into her twice more and shouted as he came. Eternity stretched out and she collapsed atop him.

Her breath slowly returned to normal as he cradled her close, caressing her spine with long, lazy strokes. She peeked up at him, flushed and sated. A rare smile curved his lips and ecstasy buoyed within her again.

He was hers.

# Chapter Seventeen

She must've fallen asleep, because Dreamer was gone and Nightmare sat near the fireplace working on a laptop when she opened her eyes.

"What time is it?" Her mind was still fogged with sleep, but she immediately searched for the clock. She didn't want to miss Shadow Mother's deadline.

He set the laptop down and rose. "It's late…a little after three in the morning."

"I'm sorry. I didn't mean to fall asleep." She sat up in bed, pressing the silk sheet to her bare skin.

"You have been through a lot in the last few days, and you were tired, there's no reason to apologize."

He waited across the room from her, not coming closer. She held her hand out to him. "Come here."

"I need a shower."

She watched him walk to the bathroom, more confused than ever. She heard the water turn on as she sat there, thinking. What caused the sudden change in Nightmare? Did he not find her attractive? Or did he want to return to Shadow Mother? Unwilling to wait idly by while he showered, she padded after him.

She slipped into the shower—large enough for a dozen people to shower together and still have room—not waiting for an invitation. Nightmare stood with his back to the door, under the showerhead, soap running down his naked body. Even though he didn't turn around, his back muscles tightened. For a moment, she stood there enjoying the way the soap bubbles slid over his body. Giving into her temptation, she ran her hands up his slippery back.

"What do you want, Kayla?" He sounded so distant, as if he didn't care.

"You."

"Only because Shadow Mother demands it." He gave her a cool look over his shoulder and pushed his face under the water.

She gently tugged his arm, pulled him closer to her. "No. I've wanted you since you showed up at Stormie's."

"That doesn't change the fact this is coming about tonight because of Shadow Mother." He took a step, advancing on her and pressing her up against the shower wall. "For a moment I thought she would not have control over me as your Enforcer in Charge, especially when it came to my sex life. But even now she controls it."

"Doesn't matter how this came about, only that it did." She ran her hands over his wet chest. "You can't deny that you want this is much as I do." She glared up at him. She wanted him and she wanted him to want her. She couldn't be wrong about his desire.

He crushed his mouth to hers, and slid his hand between her legs. Unerringly finding her core, he teased the bundle of nerves until he drew deep moans of pleasure from her. She moaned around his unrelenting kiss. He held her captive against the wall, thrusting into her with his fingers as his thumb continued to wring more pleasure from her core. Fierce desire rose within her like a tidal wave smashing through a dam.

"Nightmare, I want you." She murmured against his mouth, holding onto him as wild delight eddied through her.

His teeth grazed her lower lip and he pulled his hand away. She cried out in frustration, but he ignored her demands. Gripping her hips, he lifted her and spread her thighs before he drove into her with one powerful thrust. He gave her no time to catch her breath before he began rocking in and out of her. She had no control as he left her mouth and kissed a path to her neck. Digging her nails into his shoulders, she held on as every pump of his hips sent pulses of pleasure exploding through her. She came apart at the seams, her inner muscles clenching to him as he continued to drive into her.

He slammed home in a frenzy as his climax burst through; a second tsunami shattered her world. She shook with the force of it; where Dreamer gave her sweet ecstasy, Nightmare utterly devastated her. If it wasn't for his support she would have collapsed in a heap on the shower floor.

The water turned cold and he shut it off, sliding free of her slowly and reluctantly. Her mind was almost numb, raw sensation skittering through her. Wrapping her in a towel, he carried her out of the shower and dried her off. Her legs trembled, but she obediently followed him to bed.

Cuddled against him, her brain's misfires seemed to calm. "Why did you let Dreamer go first?" she murmured.

He turned his head to look at her and gave her an expression that said she should know, but for the life of her, she couldn't figure it out. She thought—hoped—Nightmare would be the first in her bed, but instead he ceded his place to his brother.

"If his scars repulsed you and you couldn't stand his touch, I would have returned to Shadow Mother with him."

"You thought his superficial scars would give me reason to send him to Shadow Mother?" She stared at him in shock, wondering if he really thought so little of her.

"Many have turned away from him…he lost the former Queen's favor because of them. It was just a precaution." He ran his hand through her hair. "He's the only family I have left. Since Illusion's death, we have held to each other closer than ever."

"You can't be so blind that you don't see my attraction to both of you."

"I saw it but you had never seen his scars until tonight. It was better to err on the side of caution than to risk being ordered to stay here while he returned to Shadow Mother. It's my duty as his brother to protect him." He gently pressed a soft kiss against her lips. "It's part of our culture for a Queen to sleep with many men until she's with child. I have no quarrels sharing you with Dreamer. If either of us swells your stomach with child, then I know you will be protected. But so there is no misunderstanding, I must tell you now…I will not share the bed with him or anyone else. On our nights together, it will just be us. If you have grievances with that then I'll step aside and allow you to seek whatever man you want, while I remain your Enforcer in Charge."

"There's no one I want besides you two. I trust you both with my life and if I'm to have a child, then I want it to be with one of you. Between the three of us, I know our child would be well cared for and protected."

For the first time since she'd plunged down the waterfall into the crazy, twisted Stormkin version of wonderland, she was in heaven.

# Chapter Eighteen

Kayla stood by the vanity doing her best to cover the dark circles under her eyes caused by their night of passion, while Nightmare and Dreamer discussed the day's itinerary. First they would meet with possible Enforcers and later they would attend a celebration in the town square to welcome her as Storm Hollow's new ruler.

"Kayla, are you listening?"

"Yeah." She met Dreamer's gaze in the mirror as she applied lip gloss. In truth, she hadn't been paying close attention. She heard them talking, but wasn't paying attention to the content.

"Then you agree?" he challenged.

*Shit. Of course they need a specific answer.* "No?" She drew the answer out, trying to gauge their reactions.

"You don't?" Dreamer asked, the worry clear on his face.

"Umm, sorry. Yes."

Nightmare shook his head. "You weren't listening, were you?"

"Guilty." She grimaced. "Sorry."

She could have sworn Dreamer wiped sweat from his brow. "We suggested contacting Shadow Mother before meeting the Enforcers. It would be best to inform her that you have complied with her demands."

"Oh." Grinning, she scooped her cell phone from the end table. She had no problem informing the woman that Dreamer and Nightmare were hers, period, end of story. "Yeah. Let's get it out of the way. What's her number?"

Dreamer laughed and the air caught in her throat; it was the first time she'd heard him make such a merry sound. Even faint, it was so full of life it caressed her skin making goosebumps rise on her neck.

"I apologize, my Queen." Dreamer looked down at the floor, as if afraid to meet her eyes. "Shadow Mother is contacted through the mirror, not by phone. She's too old for such modern devices."

Setting the phone down, she stepped over and caressed his cheek. "No apologies, I love your laugh." Hoping to provoke his smile again, she kissed him. She held the contact for several long seconds. "Nightmare, can you please contact Shadow Mother? Let's get it over with."

He glided to the mirror obediently. She loved the way he moved. Every step so controlled, so powerful it aroused a fresh wave of lust in her.

"Shadow Mother takes advantages of weaknesses. Step away from Dreamer…embraces show her you care and that we can be used as weapons against you. We can't afford any sign of weakness now. Not until we have gathered more Enforcers."

Reluctantly he walked closer to the mirror while Dreamer remained in place. He must have been satisfied with the distance, because he touched the mirror and said, "Shadow Mother."

The mirror swirled and a proper, neat Ginger appeared. "Ginger, Queen Kayla would like a moment of Shadow Mother's time if she's available."

"Shadow Mother is unavailable. She will return your call." The 'call' ended abruptly and the mirror smoothed over.

"I don't like it." Dreamer frowned.

"Something's amiss."

"What are you two going on about? She's busy, so what?" Kayla didn't see a cause for such concern.

"Shadow Mother should have been available. She gave you a task and only something extremely important would have deterred her from your answer. She would have been waiting for your failure or your embarrassment of bedding two men in a single night." Nightmare pulled out his cell phone.

"What caused her—" Dreamer cut himself off when Nightmare turned away, cell phone to his ear.

"Who's he calling?" She whispered.

"Windwalker…he's an unwanted. He's Earthside. No one will take him into their territory because of his power, but he has contacts. People talk to him because he has no loyalties, no one to report to. He might have an idea about what has happened concerning Shadow Mother."

"What's his power?" She walked with Dreamer, trying to offer Nightmare some privacy.

"He's actually a wind walker. He can travel by the wind and can hear anything said where the wind is moving—outside, or when a window is open." He stopped next to the window, and gazed out. "He would make a good Enforcer."

She looped her arm around his waist, and studied the activity below. People rushed around—stringing lights, erecting a large white tent, sweeping the streets, and carrying boxes and bags this way and that. Everyone was getting ready to welcome her to Storm Hollow. Hell, no one ever threw her a birthday party. *These people don't even know me, yet they seem so excited to celebrate…*

"They're doing it for you," He murmured against her temple as though reading her thoughts.

She snuggled into his body and listened to his heartbeat through his shirt. The combination of his masculine scent and spicy cologne wrapped her in security and warmth. She could stand there forever, soaking up the contact.

"What's on your mind?" He used his index finger to tilt her head up.

"I keep wondering if this is all a dream. If it is, I don't ever want to wake up. I want to stay here with both of you—forever."

He lowered his head and brushed his mouth over hers. The sweet taste of maple syrup from their breakfast lingered on his lips. "It's not a dream. Trust me, *I would know.*" He winked at her.

All her life she wanted someone to love and cherish her, now Dreamer constantly made her smile and Nightmare took her breath away.

"Windwalker has heard there was an attempt on one of Shadow Mother's Enforcers." Nightmare joined them. "That's all the information he has, but it had to be someone important to detain her from your call."

"Is there anything we can do?"

"No. If Shadow Mother needs help, she'll seek it. It's better to keep our knowledge to ourselves. We should get busy. I wrote up brief profiles for each Enforcer candidate, so we need to decide which ones, if any, you wish to interview."

She caught a glimmer of longing in Nightmare's eyes before he made his way to the bedroom sitting area. *Jealousy or something else?* She wasn't sure and they didn't have time for such complications. Dreamer tugged her after his brother.

"We were just discussing it. Would Windwalker be interested?"

"Funny you should mention it, he just made his interest plain when we were on the phone." He handed a folder to her. "I already had his profile. He's a powerful warrior. Many Queens fear his ability to hear what's said on the wind."

"His power doesn't bother me. As you said, the stronger my Enforcers are the more protection we'll have. My concern is can he be trusted? And more specifically, do you trust him?" She barely skimmed the information in the folder, preferring to hear Nightmare's opinion.

"He's an excellent warrior and would be a good addition to keep the territory safe. He's feared among all Stormkins for his ability."

She raised her eyebrows. "That dodged my question neatly."

He shot her a quick smile. "Perceptive. I have worked with him in the past and he can be trusted." He looked through the files again before handing her another one. "If we're focusing on people who can be trusted, what about Gideon?"

"Gideon? His name is…" She looked at the folder he handed her. Quickly glancing over the information.

"Gideon's not full Stormkin. His mother is Sunkin." He paused as if to give her time to let it sink in.

"A Sunkin? Aren't they the ones we're fighting…and you want me to bring him here?" Surely she was misinterpreting the advice. *This is insane.*

"He's part Sunkin which is why he's been shunned, but he's not a threat. His father raised Gideon here in Storm Hollow. When his father died a few years ago, he believed he lost his place and moved Earthside. He's not an outcast, and he's still welcome in our land. His powers are a mixture of his heritage."

She tossed the folders back onto the table and stood. A chill washed over her as she remembered Dreamer explaining his scars. How could she bring someone into Storm Hollow who had the power to blow one of them apart, to cause such horrendous scarring? To her it seemed as though they would be priming an active bomb, and waiting for it to detonate in their home.

"I don't want to risk us…any of the Stormkins of Storm Hollow."

Dreamer rose and approached the fireplace. The flames seemed to leap higher as he neared them. "It's not a risk. Gideon is a noble Enforcer…he's one of the few I'd entrust your safety to. He would protect you with his life. Meet with him and judge him for yourself. Use the same ability to see his past and his wants, like you did with Nightmare when you met him. If you can't trust our judgment, you can trust that ability."

# Chapter Nineteen

Kayla studied the fire, ignoring the files of possible Enforcers. Nightmare was working on summoning Gideon, and Dreamer left them to inspect the preparations for the evening festivities. Leaving her to mull things over.

They compared Shadow Providence to Sweetwater, only the sun didn't shine there. Beyond the windows, dark clouds floated by but it wasn't as gloomy as she imagined. The lights were bright enough to bring a warm glow.

Nightmare paced in and out of her peripheral vision. His suit jacket pulled tight across his back, the fabric moving with him. Desire warmed her blood. The longing to explore his body resurfaced with a vengeance. Politics, security issues, magic—all of that paled with the night she spent with her two men. She wanted weeks, months to explore the pleasures she shared with them.

"Gideon and Windwalker are on their way. In the meantime we should interview the others waiting downstairs." He sank down onto the sofa next to her, his focus admirable. The mirror swirled to life across the room.

"What's that?"

"A call. It's probably Shadow Mother. Come." He rose and held out his hand. At the mirror, he touched a corner and Shadow Mother appeared. Her face was contorted with anger and a touch of sadness.

"Shadow Mother, thank you for returning our call. We contacted you to—"

"Silence." Her voice cut through the air like a bullet from a high-powered rifle, holding authority and hostility before a pitcher came flying toward the window.

Kayla flinched unsure if it would come through to them or not. She opened her mouth to say something as Nightmare squeezed her wrist to remind her to tread carefully. "Shadow Mother, what can we do to help? You seem distraught."

"There has been an attack. Enforcer Bolt has been killed." Her anger vibrated in each word.

"Our sympathies, Shadow Mother. What can we do to assist you? Do you need people to search for the one responsible?" Nightmare took a step forward, doing his best to take Shadow Mother's attention and rage away from Kayla.

"Nightmare, it's good she has you to protect her. She'll need it…the path before her has become more treacherous…some will place Bolt's blood on her hands."

"On me?" Kayla paled, weakness making her knees shudder; she dared not show her fear.

"You chose our land over your father and he has sought revenge."

"What?" Tears burned behind her eyes, but she held them back.

"Nighthawk tried to demand that you be returned. He seems to be under the impression you were brought here under duress. Bolt traveled Earthside on a mission. Nighthawk waited at the portal…when Bolt came though he attacked."

She wanted to deny her father could have done it, but she couldn't get the words to come out. Her throat tightened, making it hard to breathe let alone speak.

"No disrespect intended, but how do you know it was Nighthawk?" Nightmare kept his inquiry polite.

"Bear was there. He injured Nighthawk, but was unable to kill him before he got away." Shadow Mother took a sip from a glass—probably Hurricane. She watched them with sadness in her eyes.

"Why tell us?"

"I've signed an execution warrant for him. My Enforcers are gearing up now. They'll hold for one hour. There are things he should tell Kayla himself. However, there are other ways if she doesn't wish to see him, or he won't tell her what she needs to know."

"I want to see him." Her stomach sank with Shadow Mother's words and grief overtook all other emotions. She couldn't help but feel somewhat responsible for her father's actions. "Nightmare, do we have enough time to make the trip?" She wondered how a man who'd taught her such values could be responsible for the death of at least two Enforcers. What happened to the father she'd known as a child?

"We'll leave immediately." Nightmare bowed his head to her once and returned his attention to the mirror. "Please let your Enforcers know Queen Kayla will visit Nighthawk and we'll do our best to be expedient, but they should give us time to remove her prior to their attack."

"They'll be advised. Bear will be in charge of the situation. Contact him if you're running late. Whatever you do don't let him know Enforcers have been dispatched." She leaned toward the mirror. "Queen Kayla, I wish it hadn't come to this, but he has taken things too far now. Our numbers are low and good Enforcers like Bolt are hard to come by...I can't risk any other Stormkins for the life of one outcast." The mirror returned to its opaque state, ending the call. Kayla's legs gave out beneath her.

117

She couldn't wrap her mind around it. The man who raised her with such strict beliefs…killed someone in cold blood? *How? Why?*

"Kayla." He kneeled in front of her. "I am sorry…if you want to see him we have to go now." He pulled her to her feet, shaking her once.

"Okay." Numb, she grabbed her jacket off the bed.

"Dreamer and Chameleon await us downstairs." So calm, so reserved—Nightmare handled the situation with aplomb and why shouldn't he? He hadn't just been handed his father's death warrant.

"Will we make it in time?"

"We have a portal."

Pulling on her jacket, she nodded. She glanced around the room. What else did one take to see her father for the last time? Uncertain, she headed for the door, but Nightmare barred the way.

"Are you okay?"

"Okay?" She laughed because it was better than crying. "No…my father killed a man and Shadow Mother has ordered his death. I think that's as far from okay as you can get. I understand her reasoning, and we can't have him killing people because of my decision…but he's *my father*."

Her heart was breaking as they made their way through the house to see him for the final time. She had no one to blame for this predicament save herself. If she hadn't rushed off to Shadow Providence after their fight, maybe things would have changed. He might have come around to see her side of things, or at least answered her questions. Instead, all she heard from him was silence.

By the time she descended the stairs, she was only going through the motions. She bottled everything up and locked it away. One look into Dreamer's eyes threatened to destroy her calm.

He came to her, wrapped his arms around her, and pulled her tight against him. She sank into his embrace, pressing her cheek to his crisp shirt as his cologne enfolded her like a blanket. He didn't say anything; he didn't need to. His embrace was all the comfort she needed.

She stood outside her father's house. It had been the only home she knew until she bought Stormie's. Now the familiar red brick only served to remind her of the blood her father spilled. *Why?* Why would he risk everything and kill someone they didn't know? He knew the men she'd returned to Storm Hollow with and Bolt wasn't one of them. He could have called her if he was worried for her safety.

"Kayla, you don't have to do this," Dreamer urged her; it had been his mantra since they walked through the portal.

"I do." She had to. She needed to know her father's secret. He held the answers to so many questions. Stepping onto the porch, a wave of anger struck her.

Her father jerked open the door and filled the entryway, his expression dark and foreboding. "They're not to step foot on my property. If you're returning home, they can leave."

"Dad, we need to talk."

"We have nothing to discuss until you come away from them."

"Nighthawk, she has ascended to her position, you know how this works. She goes nowhere without at least one Enforcer. I don't care if you're her father, she'll have a guard, or this conversation is over before it gets started." Nightmare was rooted firmly to her side. His words didn't surprise her because he'd told her she would not be alone with her father.

"Dad, please, I don't have a lot of time." Her voice shook, tears threatening to fall. "This is not a discussion we can have outside. The other guards can wait on the porch while Nightmare comes inside with me. If you can't agree with that then we're wasting our time and I should just leave." She held out a hand, hoping.

"No."

"Dad!" *Dammit, why can't he put his stubbornness aside for once?* She tried to push it away, not wanting the last time she saw her father to be filled with anger.

"Fine. But on the porch." He stepped out and shut the door behind him.

"I don't think this is something you want the neighborhood to hear, but if you insist." She accepted his terms and climbed the last two steps onto the porch with Nightmare in close attendance. Dreamer and Chameleon maintained their vigilance at the foot of the steps. She had twenty minutes to get the answers she wanted.

Her father chose the rocker he favored, leaving her the porch swing. He rocked silently, avoiding eye contact with her.

*Fine. Stubborn old man.* "I heard what happened." She would take the bull by the horns.

"News travels fast. I want you home."

"Dad, that wasn't the best way to get me home. You didn't need to take his life to get your point across that you're upset because I left."

He studied her men, but not her. "They took my only daughter, it's only fair I take one of their Enforcers."

This wasn't her father. Something had cracked inside of him—changed him. "What happened to you Dad? You're filled with so much anger." She hesitated, but dammit…this was her last chance. "I know what happened when you chose to leave."

"Child, you know nothing!" He glared at her. "It won't be long before you're an outcast like the rest of us."

"You can't cast out a Queen," Nightmare stated with firm conviction.

"They can when they find out what she is…" He stopped as if he'd said too much.

"What am I, Dad?" She leaned forward, focusing on him. At his continued silence, she wanted to scream, but buried the urge. *"Tell me what I am."*

He exhaled, sadness easing the stiffness of his expression. "You're part Sunkin."

# Chapter Twenty

"I'm *what?*" No way had she heard that correctly.

"Girl, have you gone deaf? I said you're part Sunkin. It's why I left…"

Her world diminished and crumbled around her. *How?*

"I was here on a mission, that's when I fell in love with your mama. I knew Shadow Mother would see it as treason. I left during the battle, hoping they'd assume I was dead." Her father seemed to deflate before her eyes.

"I know how you left and you fell in love with someone Earthside. But how am I a Sunkin?" Unable to sit still, she rose. She longed to pace, but Nightmare stood too close.

"Everyone goes through a streak where they do everything their parents don't want them to. I was your mama's. She expected it to be a quick fling to upset her father, but she became pregnant with you. I loved her and talked her into marrying me. Shortly after you were born and she realized your abilities were darker than her *perfect* Sunkin ones, she returned to her homeland. Your mother is a Sunkin princess." There was a strong note of bitterness in his voice, but she wasn't sure whether it was because he'd been left to raise her alone or because she was able to return to her people when he couldn't.

She sat down, dumbfounded. How did they manage to meet let alone fall in love when they were on different sides? No wonder he snuck off.

From what she'd seen of Shadow Mother she would've never allowed him to leave to be with the enemy.

"A princess? Is that really possible?"

Nightmare shot her a brief smile before his expression turned unreadable again. "Leave it to you, my Queen, to question that…instead of asking who she is. The Sunkins' land is different than ours, one family rules everyone. They have a King, and when he dies someone else in his royal bloodline steps into place."

"Come. There's something inside you should have." Her father rose and started toward the door, not bothering to see if she followed.

She waited for Nightmare's nod and they stepped inside together. Her father's home appeared as it always had, but now the air in the house seemed denser, making it harder to breathe. With each step, the fog around her grew heavier. Nightmare reached out, wrapping his arm around her, throwing them to the floor. A package dropped, landing next to her with a thump.

"Dreamer!" Nightmare howled. A large hawk headed straight for them.

Dreamer rushed in, sword drawn, while Nightmare scooted her away as if the package might explode. The hawk had to be her father; she wasn't sure how she knew, but she did. Everything played out before she had time to fully process it.

The hawk flew out the door and gunshots echoed through the air. *Dad.* Her mind screamed and her heart sank, her father's death—so abstract before—was sudden, painfully real.

Somehow she ended up on the sofa curled into a ball as her body shook uncontrollably. Her stomach twisted into knots as she waited for the horrible reality to be confirmed. Every passing moment brought fresh, uncontrollable chills.

Nightmare stood close, examining the box her father dropped next to her on the floor. She reached for the afghan that laid on the back of the sofa, hoping to ward off the worst of the chill, when Dreamer's voice rose in the distance. The scuffle drew Nightmare's attention; he slipped the small box into his pocket, his gaze on the hallway. He didn't leave her, as if he knew Dreamer and Chameleon had it under control.

"She had nothing to do with this. Leave her be," Dreamer said from the other side of the room where he stood guard at the doorway.

"Get out of the way or I'll move you." A large man made his way to the sofa with Dreamer a step behind. "Queen Kayla, Mother Shadow gave you a direct order not to warn Nighthawk."

Nightmare stood in front of her blocking the other's approach.

"Bear, she had nothing to do with this. I was with her." Nightmare's voice was steady, controlled.

"I need some damn answers and I need them now." The other man growled.

"Bear, she's in shock, give her a moment. She thinks your team just killed her father." Dreamer's words seemed to come from a great distance. *Does that mean they didn't kill my father?* "Chameleon, see if you can find her something warm to drink, tea would be best to help ward off the shock."

Bear stormed from the room and she didn't care where he went or why. Every blink rasped fresh sandpaper against her eyes.

"My Queen." Dreamer sank to his knees in front of her, and placed his hand over hers. "Look at me, Kayla."

The first tear splashed down her cheek as she met Dreamer's sympathetic eyes. Her father's crimes didn't seem to matter anymore. With him gone, she was an orphan. "He's…"

"No. He escaped. He was not killed."

Chameleon reappeared and pressed a hot mug into her hands. "Drink this, my Queen, it will warm you. I've added honey to it."

She wrapped her hands around the mug as she would a life raft, and inhaled the spicy aroma of the chai tea her father always kept on hand for her visits.

*Escaped. He got away.*

With each sip her mind cleared, and she had to get away from this house. She couldn't sit there being surrounded by her father's things, by their memories any longer. "I want to go home."

"We need to speak with…" He paused when Bear walked into the room. "Queen Kayla, this is Bear, Shadow Mother's Enforcer in Charge. He needs to talk to you."

"Queen Kayla." He nodded his head and paused at the edge of the sofa. "There's no need. Shadow Mother has requested we follow his trail but leave you out of it. She believes you had nothing to do with his disappearance."

"Good because I had *nothing* to do with it." She needed to defend herself.

He shook his head and waved the others out, and the room emptied of everyone except her guards. "I won't be back here…I need to gather a few things before we leave." She looked around the room. This would never again be home, at least not the home she grew up in. Somewhere, somehow—that door to her past closed and would never open again.

Back in Storm Hollow, she shut herself in her bedroom, under the pretense she wanted to unpack the things she brought back from her father's home. In truth, she needed to be alone, needed time to adjust to the knowledge she would—could—never see her father again. At least he was still alive. She also had to think about the bomb her father dropped; she was a Sunkin. She was worried that since she'd just lost her father she'd also lose her place here, and more importantly her men.

She had nothing left back in her world so it was time to make Storm Hollow a true home. Looking out over her town, the lights below reminded her of a small city, yet it didn't seem like enough. She wanted more, she wanted it to feel like the home she'd just lost, but the only warmth Storm Hollow offered so far was Nightmare and Dreamer.

She placed a picture of her and her father taken when she was six, during a father daughter dance on the nightstand. It was one of her favorite pictures of them. The night played out clearly in her mind, even after all those years. That night she felt like a princess. Their neighbor loved to sew and made her a custom dress for the dance, it was everything she wanted and more.

A knock woke her from her memories. The door opened and Dreamer leaned inside. "You okay?"

She nodded, afraid if she spoke that her voice would betray her. He glided across the large room in a matter of seconds and swept her into his arms. Carrying her to the sofa, he nuzzled her forehead. "I'm sorry. I know it's hard."

On the sofa, she snuggled into him. He gently rubbed his hand over her back, soothing her, as the tears fell. "I know he's not…dead…but…"

He rubbed her back. "Shh, baby. It feels the same way. You've lost him, and you're grieving. That's nothing to be ashamed of."

She wasn't sure how long they stayed like that but her eyes were growing heavy when the door opened again.

"It's only me," Nightmare called, shutting the door quietly. Her eyes were still closed when the space on the sofa next to her sank under his bulk. "I have the box your father left." He sat it in her lap.

The creamy white box laid like a brick on her thighs. She stared down at it and ran her hand over the box. The smooth heavy cardboard was cool under her fingers. Biting the inside of her cheek, she slid the lid open. Inside on a layer of cotton laid a silver bracelet with a yellow and orange swirl sun charm. Her fingers played over the charm. Her head was still against Dreamer's chest, making her all too aware of his deep breath when she opened the box. "What is it?" When Dreamer didn't answer she turned her gaze toward Nightmare.

"It's a royal Sunkin bracelet. Only those of the royal line have them. There's a message underneath."

Her heart raced as she lifted the bracelet to free the note beneath. Her fingers trembled when she unfolded the paper. In curly handwriting, she read the following words.

*Someday I hope Nighthawk will explain why I could not stay. Please don't hate me, for it's what was best. When you're ready to forgive, come, and take your rightful place among the true court. Leave Nighthawk and any he may have exposed you to. Join me in the kingdom of the pure. Your mother, Raye.*

Hate her...*you have to love someone before you can hate them*. Her father's advice whispered in her mind. At that moment she wasn't completely sure because she had some mighty strong feelings for her, all of them in the negative category. How could someone have a child and just leave them?

Nightmare's voice drew her from her thoughts. "There's something more on the back."

She flipped the paper over and the other side held her father's handwriting, short and to the point just like he was. *She was a good woman but had a selfish streak a mile wide. Don't think for a second you would be safe in Raye's world. Nightmare and Dreamer are good men, they'll protect you as long as they let go of their hatred for me. I'll be fine. Everything I did was to protect you. Shadow Mother knew this day would come. She visited shortly after your mother left. I thought she'd come to kill*

128

*me herself, but that wasn't her way. She's been waiting for you. The ring you wear on your finger is from her. You'll need it on your journey. You're to be the next Shadow Providence ruler—the next Shadow Mother. It's been an honor to be your father, to raise you to become the ruler of our people. Be safe. I love you.*

Her mind raced. *The next Shadow Mother?* He couldn't be serious. She forced the page at Nightmare, her hands shaking worse than before. "What the hell does *that* mean?"

# Chapter Twenty-One

"It means what it says. You'll rule over this land as Shadow Mother one day if you make the changes that need to be made. Without you our world will continue to fall into torment until we are all but extinct. You'll turn our people around, make us stronger." Nightmare explained, while he gently rubbed her leg. "During my time working under Shadow Mother I've been able to learn more about the prophecies than others. She has known this would happen for years and we've been preparing."

"All the while taking the Sunkins—my mother's people—down." There was no anger in her voice, it was just a statement.

"You were raised Earthside, do you want to see that land gone? Your family, friends, vanished? If we let the Sunkins go on as they have, in five years there'll be nothing left of your world. You have to realize that."

"I guess I never thought of it like that. All of this is so new...I never expected this battle to keep humans safe and I surely never thought I would be a part of it. It's just too much. What if I can't do it?" She let her head fall back on Dreamer's chest and closed her eyes.

"I understand it's a lot of pressure, and a complete change from the life you're used to. If anyone can do it, you can." He squeezed her thigh. "We'll be there, doing whatever we can to help you. But you can do it. Have faith in yourself."

She listened to Dreamer's heartbeat, wishing she had the faith in herself that they seemed to have in her. It would make things so much easier, and she could stop doubting herself.

"You're not thinking of leaving us to…" Dreamer started to ask but couldn't finish. It was clear from the stiffness in his body he wondered if she would go to the land of the Sunkins and leave them behind. She wanted to stay right where she was.

She raised her hand to his cheek. "Oh, Dreamer. I'm not leaving. This is my home now. She left me as a child because my abilities were too dark for her, I'm sure nothing has changed. Even so, I'm not going anywhere."

"Your abilities…" Nightmare began. "That explains where your telekinesis comes from."

"What?" They both asked together.

"Telekinesis is customarily a Sunkin power."

The weight of his words hung in the air like heartburn from spicy food. *Why didn't Shadow Mother tell me this? Will my mixed heritage cause more problems when it becomes known to the other Queens? I can't lose the only place I have left.* Her father's words played in her mind again… *They'll outcast her when they find out what she is. If I become an outcast from Shadow Providence where would I go? I can't return to Sweetwater without Dad.*

"Does this change anything? Will I not be welcomed here because…"

"Shadow Mother already knew before she welcomed you to our land. Nothing has changed. I believe it might be your mixed heritage that will allow you to complete the tasks that lie ahead. Either way, your power of telekinesis is something to be cherished. We'll work with you to hone your abilities."

"You're tired. Why don't you lie down? I need to go check on the setup for tonight." Dreamer slid her to the side and stood up. Immediately she missed his touch, his warmth. She watched him grab his suit jacket from the back of the couch before he made his way across the room. Alone with Nightmare she missed the ease Dreamer brought to the room. Nightmare, her hardened warrior, always seemed on edge.

"You should listen to him. You had a long night."

She rose, stretching her body as she stood. "Are you staying?"

"Do you want me to stay?"

Yes, she wanted him there, but as always he avoided a direct answer. She still had doubts as to why they were in her bed. She hated the thought of them only being there because she was their ruler, and they wanted to make her happy. She didn't want them there out of duty…but because they genuinely wanted to be.

"Lay with me…at least until I fall asleep." She added the last bit so he didn't feel required to stay.

"I thought you'd never ask." He slipped his hand into hers. "You worry too much my sweet Kayla."

Dreamer stepped out of the SUV onto Main Street to find that things were coming together. Lights were strung up, leading in the direction of the large white tent that was erected in the center of town. The town bustled with people rushing around with balloons, chairs, and tables. Everyone was in full swing for the festivities.

"Dreamer…" Breezy rushed toward him. He was surprised how much she had changed over the last few years. In the time they had been away, she had gone from a child to a beautiful woman. Her long brown hair flowed freely behind her, her plain figure turned curvy.

"Breezy." He wrapped his arms around her drawing her into a hug. "It's so good to see you again." Her vanilla scent engulfed him, reminding him of

133

yesteryear.

She kissed his cheek. "I've missed you. I heard Nightmare's home as well."

"Yes. He's with the Queen, but he'll be here tonight."

She smiled at him before giving him another hug. "I've got to get back to the shop. I'm in charge of desserts. I'll see you tonight and we can catch up. I've missed you so much."

*Shop?* She was off before he had time to gather his wits. Since arriving back in Storm Hollow he had been both eager and apprehensive about seeing Breezy again, not knowing what her reaction would be. Now he could put those worries to rest and focus on his duties.

He strolled through the area closed off for the celebration, checking the number of cleared exits should they need to evacuate the Queen. He directed the men setting up the tables to move the ones closest to the one reserved for Kayla back another five feet when Chameleon found him.

*What's he doing down here?*

Chameleon drew close and scanned the area to make sure they wouldn't be overheard. "Thunder is demanding to see Queen Kayla."

"We've been expecting his decision. She's busy now. Let him know she'll see him soon. In the meantime he can stay in the barracks." He gave the area another once over. "I'm heading back, want a ride?"

The Enforcer nodded and followed Dreamer toward the parked SUV. "Thunder has been a good Enforcer over the years, I'm surprised he hasn't pledged his loyalties to Kayla."

That bugged Dreamer as well. Thunder had always been a good Enforcer and had remained loyal even after Nighthawk was exiled. Why hadn't he pledged his loyalties to Kayla initially…unless he was a traitor to their people?

Kayla woke slowly, still deeply snuggled against Nightmare. His cologne tantalized her as she clung to him. Not wanting to disturb his peaceful sleep, she took advantage of the opportunity to study him. His chest gently rose and fell in a soothing rhythm.

She wished for the peace he had in his sleep. Her dreams were plagued with images of her father—he blamed her for his need to flee—and of a woman whose face she couldn't see but she had a distinct feeling it was her mother. Hatred and rage charged her dreams and left a tingle of fear in their wake.

Her decision to return to Shadow Providence with Nightmare and Dreamer pushed her father to the breaking point. Would she have made the same decision if she had known of her heritage? She couldn't be sure, but the knowledge made her current decisions harder. Should she try to hide the fact she was part Sunkin?

Nightmare woke to find Kayla resting her head against his chest. "Too much on your mind to sleep?" he murmured, stroking her arm.

She looked up at him, a feeble smile trembling on her lips. "I slept...for a bit."

"Not long enough." He tucked a strand of her blonde hair behind her ear to give him a clear view of her eyes. "What are you thinking of, my Queen?"

He watched her lips curl down in a frown when he said *my Queen*. It was beyond him why she detested those two little words; it was her identity and he'd serve her until his final breath. She was the one he had waited for. The one who would change everything. It was an honor to serve as her Enforcer in Charge.

"A little of this and that," she mumbled.

He ran a finger down her cheekbone, to her jaw, and back up. "My sweet Kayla, I long to take away the agony in your eyes. You deserve so much." He kissed her softly, and took her bottom lip into his mouth. With each kiss, he wanted more of her. She tasted of sweet vanilla with a splash of spice. He desired her, all of her.

He glided his hands over her body, as each kiss grew more forceful. Carefully, he pushed her onto her back. Slipping out of his clothes, he rose above her. "I've waited for you my whole life and I'm not letting you go now that I have you."

Grasping the hem of her nightshirt, he tugged it up over her head. He tossed it over the side of the bed to lay next to his discarded clothes, before turning his attention to her nipples. They stood at attention with anticipation. Lowering his head, he drew lazy circles around each hardened bud before drawing one into his mouth. She writhed under him as he took his time with each one.

Abandoning the puckered tip, he trailed kisses to her earlobe, tantalizing her with each nibble. Every touch amped up his violent want of her.

"Nightmare please," she whispered, her breath hot against his neck.

"Please, what? Take my time?" He teased.

"Nightmare," she growled, demanding.

Without further delay, he thrust his shaft into her warm center. The air crackled around them as if it had been waiting for that moment when their bodies joined together as one. Her inner muscles clamped down on him greedily as he worked his way in and out of her. It didn't take long to find the rhythm that bound them together.

Waves of ecstasy flooded through him. She squirmed beneath him as she neared her apex. She dug her fingers into his back and she arched into him.

Wild pleasure filled him to a breaking point; he threw his head back as he slammed home one final time and his cry joined hers in release.

Collapsing, he rolled onto his side and nuzzled her damp forehead. He loved this woman—utterly—Queen or not. Enforcers shouldn't fall in love with their Queens. Love clouded judgment and hampered their ability to protect.

He silently vowed to protect her. To him, being in love with her was all the more reason he was the best person to keep her safe.

# Chapter Twenty-Two

A knock forced Kayla from Nightmare's arms. She pushed herself to her elbow and stared bleary-eyed at the door. "My Queen…" Dreamer called before he cracked the door an inch.

"Come in." She sighed and fell back against the pillows.

If discovering her intimacy with Nightmare bothered him, he didn't show it. "Thunder has requested a moment of your time."

"It's about time. He better have a decision or he can be remanded into custody until the next council meeting." Nightmare drew lazy circles on her shoulder with his fingers.

"Chameleon said it's important, so I would assume he's come to a decision. Are you sure he can be trusted?" Dreamer approached the bed.

"I believe he can be, but until we know for sure he'll be closely supervised, and won't be allowed alone with Kayla." Nightmare curled an arm beneath his head, his expression quiet, and thoughtful. "Bring him to the conference room. We'll be there shortly."

The last thing she wanted was another meeting with someone bearing yet another grudge. She wasn't ready to face Thunder or anyone else for that matter. Too bad that wasn't an option. Destiny didn't appear willing to wait. Resigned, she tossed back the comforter, and went in search of her clothes.

Silence filled the room as she slipped on the jeans and blouse she had on earlier. "You told him you thought Thunder could be trusted. Are you sure? He went behind Shadow Mother's back for years to visit my father. She could do more to him than I could, and yet he risked it."

"Shadow Mother had to have known, yet she did nothing. Apparently, she visited your father herself. All that has happened must be part of the prophecy." He dressed faster than she did and looked far less rumpled.

"Why don't we ask?"

"If she didn't know, it would be signing his death warrant. Is that what you want?"

She swallowed hard trying not to be offended. "I don't want that." She just wanted to understand why he would risk everything, daring Shadow Mother's wrath.

"He's waiting." He guided her to the door.

Her heels clicked on the dark wood floor as they made their way down the long corridor from their rooms toward the conference room. Trying to focus on something other than the man she would be meeting, she took in her surroundings. The walls were a pale gold that brought out the shine of the wood floors. The hallway was lined with expensive looking art, and each room they passed contained antiques. None of it particularly her taste but she could appreciate the beauty of it.

Chameleon stood guard outside the conference room and he opened the doors at her approach. "My Queen." He bowed his head as she passed. Dreamer waited inside, his gaze fixed on Thunder almost as if he expected the man to attack.

The prospective Enforcer sat directly on the other side of the long mahogany conference table. She laid her hand on top of a leather chair, and watched him for a long moment. "You've come to a decision?"

Thunder nodded. "I wish to serve you, my Queen."

"How do I know I can trust you?"

"I have risked everything to…" He stopped almost as quickly as he started and smacked his hand onto the table. The bang brought Dreamer away from the wall and to her side.

"What? You want me to trust you, then tell me." She'd had enough of half-truths and lies told to *protect* her.

"My father was able to see into the future. He told me Nighthawk would be the one to bring life to our people. It wasn't until he left that I realized he meant Nighthawk would bring life *back* to our people. You'll restore us to what we once were and bring fertility to our land again. Nighthawk was an outcast but I wanted to see that you were safe, that you knew of our kind. The last time I came to visit, Nighthawk and I had an intense argument. I thought the time had come to tell you what you were, to help you embrace your abilities. Instead your father wanted to suppress them. He did his best to shelter you. He never told you what you were or about your destiny. He once mentioned he had no loyalties to help his people since he was cast out of his homeland."

"Dad made me feel like a freak, especially when it came to the telekinesis. Why didn't you tell me?" Sadness filled her. Her father's anger was the worst when she couldn't keep her abilities hidden.

"The telekinesis wasn't something Nighthawk was used to dealing with. I didn't tell you for fear your father would take you into hiding. In Sweetwater, I could watch over you. I had hoped I would be able to find you when you were ready and bring you home. I couldn't have brought you here until you were able to defend yourself. You needed to come as a Queen, completely in your powers." Thunder leaned forward in his chair. "It was all part of the prophecy. It could have altered your destiny if I interfered."

*Telekinesis wasn't something he was used to dealing with.* Anger stewed under the surface like water ready to boil over. "You mean because telekinesis is a Sunkin ability? What the hell did he think would happen when he conceived a child with a Sunkin? That I would have none of her abilities?"

He looked from Nightmare to Dreamer as if seeking help, but they said nothing.

"Yes, my Queen, it's a Sunkin ability. Why he reacted the way he did is only something he can answer. What you need to remember is he loved you regardless of your abilities. I believe he was just concerned for your safety should those abilities be brought to light."

She was through discussing her father and his choices. She had her own to make. "Why do you want to serve as my Enforcer now, when yesterday you couldn't get away fast enough?"

He flinched as if she'd hit him. "It wasn't that I didn't wish to pledge my commitment to you last evening, I was concerned my pledge would bring my visits to Sweetwater to Shadow Mother's attention and she would call for my death. Then I realized there's nothing that can be done if it's my time. But while I'm here I want to make sure you're safe."

She looked to Nightmare. Did he believe Thunder? She wanted to, but they couldn't afford a misstep.

"Touch him," Nightmare whispered as he pulled out the chair.

"It doesn't always work on command."

"You can do it." He gave her shoulder a gentle rub and eyed Thunder. "Give the Queen your hand."

The man slid his hand across the table without any questions. With a deep breath, she cleared her mind, and grasped his hand. His fingers were warm against hers and images flashed in her mind. Visions of him sneaking around to visit her and the argument with Nighthawk. Both confirmed his story. He had watched over her all her life, even after he stopped visiting

Nighthawk. He had a fatherly love for her. Then she caught something else—a hint of betrayal.

"You..." she stammered as she pulled away from him. She rubbed her hand as if she'd been burnt. Disbelief washed over her. "You, you attacked her..."

"Who?" Dreamer asked, before he placed his hand on her shoulder.

"The woman who gave birth to me. Why?"

"She was leaving while Nighthawk was at work. She planned to take you back to the Sunkin land. Your father would have never seen you again and our people would have lost everything. She only wanted you because he told her the prophecy. I just wanted to stop her from leaving, from taking you. I wanted to save you—save our kind." No guilt marred the truth in his voice.

"Wait in the hall with Chameleon. Queen Kayla needs a few minutes to make her decision." Nightmare nodded to the door.

Thunder stood, his gaze still locked on hers. "My Queen, when you were born I vowed to protect you. I knew then what you would bring to our people, but that wasn't the reason for my vow. I did it because Nighthawk was like a brother to me and over the years I've spent watching you, you've almost became like the daughter I never had. Nothing has changed on my end, I'll protect you with my dying breath."

The door clicked shut behind him and left an impenetrable silence in his wake. His words played through her mind. What he said was the truth, yet she couldn't shake the feeling he hadn't been completely upfront with her.

"Did you find the answers you seek?" Dreamer sat down next to her.

"He's been truthful. I understand the reason behind his attack on Raye. He'll pledge his oath to me, but the first time he goes against my orders that will be it."

The fact he attacked her birth mother didn't bother her, but something else did—something she couldn't name. Her life could have been very different if he had allowed Raye to take her—maybe better, maybe worse—but he held back on something and until she knew what it was, she refused to trust him. Nightmare seemed to, and that would have to do for now.

# Chapter Twenty-Three

Kayla made her way through the crowd of Storm Hollow residents to the center, where a special table awaited her. All of her Enforcers—all four of them—moved with her. The lights strung throughout Main Street brought a warm glow to the tent. Food lined the length of the pavilion, each item looking more delicious than the last. A separate dessert table sat in the corner lined with cakes, cookies, pies and, her favorite, a chocolate waterfall along with platters of assorted items to dip in the succulent melted sweet.

"My Queen, welcome to Storm Hollow. Please help yourself." A woman with long raven black hair bowed her head to Kayla. When she looked up her emerald green eyes shimmered with light.

"Queen Kayla, this is Icy, she's the owner of Storm Hollow Café. She was in charge of putting this celebration together, as well as preparing the food," Nightmare said by way of introduction.

"I can't take complete responsibility. I wouldn't have been able to pull this off without Breezy, especially her enchanting desserts. She'll be glad you're home. Please eat while the food is hot, we'll have time to talk later. If you need anything I'll be around." Icy bowed again and disappeared into the crowd.

"Who's Breezy?" Kayla quietly asked him as she added a piece of the grilled chicken breast to her plate.

"Now's not the time." He did a quick scan to see if anyone might be listening, then forked a steak from the platter and added it to his dish. "At our table."

She added a bit of this and that to her plate, before they walked through the crowd to their table. *Why so secretive about this woman? Does he have feelings for her?* Jealousy coursed through her veins, and then the truth hit her like a lighting strike. She was in love with him.

At the table, the brothers each took a seat on either side of her before Nightmare slipped a small black stone out of his pocket. He looked around the room before he blew on it to make it glow a soft blue, creating a privacy shield.

"We were just entering Enforcer training when our mother passed. A few years later our father remarried...Breezy is our half-sister. We've done our best to keep it quiet, so as not to put her in danger, especially after what happened here before." Nightmare's plate sat untouched as he told her the story, his gaze fluttering between her, Breezy, and the rest of the Stormkins who had gathered for the celebration.

*Sister.* The corners of her lips turned upward into a smile, with the news Breezy was not a woman she had to compete with. "Does she know?"

"Yes. We were close before we had to leave Storm Hollow. She was young then, I suspect she has forgotten about us by now."

"She hasn't." Dreamer spoke up from her other side where he had been quietly listening as he ate. "I bumped into her while supervising setting up. She's looking forward to seeing you. She opened her own shop, Stormy Treats."

"Why didn't you tell me?" Nightmare asked, eyeing his brother.

"When I got back you were entertained, and we were busy dealing with another issue." It was understood the other issue was Thunder.

146

"I'll make time to seek her out later." Nightmare nodded. "My Queen, after you eat, there are two potential Enforcers I would like to introduce you to."

*Yay—more stress.* Nightmare removed the privacy shield. They made small talk as they ate, taking the time to discuss different members of Storm Hollow, and business. To her surprise her territory was larger than she thought. There were almost eight hundred Stormkins living in Storm Hollow, and according to Nightmare the number would only grow as their community became the safe haven for half-breeds and unwanted Stormkins.

"My Queen, I've put together a sample platter of all the best desserts especially for you and your Enforcers." A woman with the same chestnut brown hair as Nightmare and Dreamer placed a large gold platter before her. Each dessert looked delicious, but she wasn't sure she could eat another thing.

"This is Breezy, the owner of Stormy Treats," Dreamer told her, smiling up at the woman.

"Breezy, it's nice to meet you. Thank you for the desserts. Tomorrow come to the main house for lunch." Kayla reached for a chocolate-covered strawberry.

"Yes, my Queen. Thank you." She bowed her head slightly, before turning to Nightmare. "I'm glad you're home."

"Why did you invite her?" Nightmare asked after Breezy had stepped away from them.

She leaned close, pressing her lips almost against his ear. "I thought you'd like to spend some time privately with her. This way you won't have to worry about your secret getting out. No one would suspect she didn't come to see me. It will give you an opportunity to reconnect with her." She nibbled on her strawberry, content she'd done something to repay her men.

"If anyone finds out who she is, they could kill her to get back at us. She'll be in danger if our relationship is ever known."

"Are you telling me you'd rather I didn't invite her? That you would rather be this close but have no contact with her?" When he didn't answer, she added, "We'll protect her. Storm Hollow is going to be a safe place, remember?"

For once, it was her men who didn't seem convinced. She loved Nightmare and Dreamer, that meant she'd make sure Breezy was safe. *If Breezy's here in Storm Hollow, are their parents still here as well?*

"Where are your father and her mother?" She quietly whispered to Nightmare.

"In another territory. They were transferred when Queen Lisa took over, but Breezy chose to say behind." He glanced about to make sure they weren't over heard.

"Since you're done eating, we should meet the possible Enforcers." He rose, and put his hand out for her. "Dreamer, with us. Chameleon and Thunder, we'll be back."

"Okay." She mumbled as she rose. Instead of meeting possible Enforcers, she wanted to mingle with the residents and have a good time.

"It won't be long and then how about a dance?" Dreamer placed his hand on the small of her back.

She smiled back at him and gave him a quick nod before following Nightmare. Mostly everyone was still at their tables, nibbling on desserts. The soft music played throughout the area as a few people made their way to the dance floor at the far end.

Nightmare led them off to the side where two men stood talking together. At their arrival, the men grew quiet. "Queen Kayla, this is Mist."

The shorter one with pale white hair brushed the top of his suit jacket and held out his hand. "My Queen." He bowed his head as he brought her hand to his lips. When he raised his head, all she could see were his eyes. They were pale as the clouds, and drew her in.

"Storm," Nightmare said, providing the jolt she needed to free herself from Mist's gaze.

Storm was taller than Mist. His muscles more defined under the suit, his hair a complete contrast to Mist, black as night, and had a slight wave to it. At first glance she thought the side of his neck had a tattoo of a lightning bolt, but on closer inspection she could see that it appeared to be more of a brand.

"Storm was an unwanted from Queen Lisa's territory and sent to live here when his abilities became something she feared. She didn't see Storm as an asset to assist her in ruling her territory, only someone who could ruin everything she gained. Men do not rule in Shadow Providence but that doesn't mean they should be any less feared. A strong Enforcer against his Queen can turn others, and eventually she could lose the land she ruled. Mist completed the Enforcers' training, but has never been promoted." Nightmare clasped his hands in front of his belt buckle.

"My Queen, I understand if you wish for me to leave your territory, but my sister Icy...I beg you to allow her to remain in her home, she has a business here. Icy has never caused any problems." Storm bowed his head to her and she found it respectable that he was more concerned for his sister than himself.

"Storm, do I have any reason to fear you?" she asked.

Nightmare wouldn't waste her time if he thought of Storm as a threat. If Nightmare wasn't concerned, then she saw no reason to be either.

"No, my Queen. As I told Nightmare, I would be honored to pledge my loyalty to you."

"Very well. Then you have nothing to worry about, Icy will be safe. Come with me and we'll talk." Before she turned to leave she studied Mist again. "Mist, we can use good Enforcers. Come to the main house in the morning and we'll discuss your future in Storm Hollow."

"Yes, my Queen."

Soft music filled the evening air, while Nightmare held Kayla tight in his arms. They danced as if unconcerned about any lurking dangers. But he was on alert, even though he seemed relaxed with her in his arms. He watched for anything or anyone that could cause her harm while her other Enforcers stood nearby.

"Are you all right? You seem preoccupied."

"I had a wonderful time tonight. It was an amazing celebration….but I'm tired."

"That was all you needed to say. We'll leave." He guided her off the dance floor and motioned to his brother. "We're leaving."

Dreamer nodded before he motioned to Chameleon and Thunder. "Breezy sent a box of the chocolate covered strawberries you seemed to favor," he explained as Thunder headed toward them with a box in hand.

"Where is she? I should thank her."

"She's already gone. She gets up early for the bakery and didn't want to interrupt your dance. You'll see her tomorrow." Dreamer laid his hand on her arm. "Let's go home."

As they made their way to the SUV, someone came rushing toward them. Dreamer pushed her behind him and the four men tightened their circle around her, making her slightly claustrophobic. Their hands went for their weapons. She couldn't get a good glimpse of who approached, but the tension around her continued to climb.

"Stand down, it's Windwalker," Nightmare told the Enforcers. "Windwalker, what's the meaning of this?"

"Shadow Mother, she's been trying to reach you. You must come quickly, or she has threatened to come here tonight."

"It must be a matter of urgency because she knows tonight's the celebration." Nightmare adjusted enough to look back at Kayla. "You didn't have time to question Windwalker, but if he has not committed his vow to you, Shadow Mother can demand he return to her."

"Windwalker, did you bring the second SUV?" When he nodded, she turned to the other men. "Chameleon, Thunder take that. Unless something happens, you're off duty. Get some rest." Moving her attention back to Windwalker, she didn't have time to fancy foot around the issue at hand. She just dove in headfirst with the questions. "Why do other Queens fear you? Have you done anything to become unwanted?"

"I like that you come straight to the point," Windwalker said as they climbed into the SUV. He rode in the back with her, so they could have their discussion on the drive back to the main house. "It's my ability that causes their alarm, not me. I can travel on the wind, but I can also hear what's said when there's any kind of wind. Queens are concerned I'll betray them if I know their dark secrets or strategies."

"It makes sense they would fear this unless you were one of the trusted Enforcers." She looked to Nightmare and longed to be able to read him. Nightmare brought him to Storm Hollow, which led her to believe he trusted him. His abilities weren't without risk but they could prove extremely valuable if all the unrest they kept warning her about came true. "Give me your hand."

Without hesitation, he did as she asked which gave him a bonus point in her book. She focused with the intent to see the truth as she asked the next set of questions. "Do you want to serve me and if so do I have any reason to fear you?"

"I, like so many others, have waited for you. It would be an honor to serve you. Once I give my vow, I will never take it back. My service would be to you and only you."

The truth of his answers caressed her skin, like the tidal flow of sun-heated water. He didn't answer if she had reason to fear her. Despite her earlier reticence to use her abilities, she wholeheartedly embraced them. They belonged to her and like the blind woman given her first glimpse of the light, the results were addicting. She wanted to know why he refused the earlier answer.

She pushed away the memories of things she didn't need—missions, celebrations, and punishments—until she found it. *Enemies.* He thought she should be worried of his enemies, *not* of him.

# Chapter Twenty-Four

Kayla and Nightmare had barely made it to her bedroom when the mirror began to swirl with a call. She took a deep breath as he laid his hand on the corner of the mirror. Shadow Mother filled the glass, glaring at them as though they had inexplicably failed her.

"Shadow Mother, we were just about to contact you." He angled himself slightly in front of Kayla.

"While you have been out celebrating I've been dealing with the Sunkin King."

"Shadow Mother—"

"Don't. The Sunkin King demands the return of his Princess. According to that ignorant bastard, she has been kidnapped, and that's the reason she's here." Her hands formed into tight balls, as she let out a sound that sent chills up Kayla's spine. "Nightmare, talk to Queen Kayla, explain who the Sunkin are and that if she chooses them what will happen to our people."

*Tread carefully. Remember her temper.* "Shadow Mother, he has already explained who they are. I'm not leaving, this is my home now."

"Very well. Contact Sunkin King and let him know your decision. However, know this…if you leave I'll see that the men you've bedded suffer. You'll be a traitor to our kind and they'll suffer for your treason." With that, the mirror became solid again.

Her fingertips burned with the anger coursing through her. She tried to calm herself, to put a lid on her emotions before they got out of control and lightning shot from her fingertips again. *I'm tired of these games she's playing. How dare she threaten me with the lives of my men to get her way.*

"Threatening me won't get her very far, it only pisses me off." She reached for Nightmare, her legs a little wobbly. The idea of him suffering for a decision she made was unthinkable.

"You can't go against her." His lifted her into his arms as if she weighed nothing, and made his way to the bed and sat her on it. "Nothing's going to happen to us. Shadow Mother's just upset. She has been trying to defeat the Sunkins for years. Now that you have joined us, she finally has a chance. No matter her faults, one thing is for sure, she's aware they can offer you things she cannot. They might not be better, just different things, like the sun."

"I have what I want." She ran her hand over his cheek. She wanted to feel his five o'clock shadow under her fingers.

"Then let us deal with the situation." He took hold of her hand, bringing it to his lips. "It will be fine. I want Dreamer with us for this call."

*Can I really protect them all?* What if they were wrong in choosing her? What if their faith in her was utterly misplaced?

"Dreamer's on his way. In the meantime, you need to know that your mother might be there when we place this call. Are you ready for that?" He knelt in front of her, gathering her hands in his.

"I'll be fine. Raye was never a mother to me. As far as I'm concerned she's just another stranger in a sea of outsiders. I figured I'd have to face her at some point. It's best to get it over with."

He kissed her before he stood, still holding her hand; his touch was like a cool summer rain. Dreamer joined them and claimed her free hand.

"There's nothing to worry over, I'm not going to the Sunkin land. I will

154

not leave you two. Let's get this over with. I'm tired." She could sleep for a year. Two days in this world and she had never been more exhausted.

Nightmare let go of her hand and stepped toward the mirror. "Stand together, it will give us a stronger presence. If you find a weakness, use it to your benefit. Kayla, we'll remain silent at your sides unless you need us. If they don't wish to use your title, which they should out of respect, then you're under no obligation to use theirs. Last thing and take it as you will, Raye *will* take offense to you not calling her mother."

She nodded, squeezed Dreamer's hand gently, then let go as the mirror began to swirl.

A man appeared in a gold dress shirt and white slacks. His short pale blond hair made his blue eyes more vibrant. "Sunkin King Lucian, Queen Kayla of the Stormkins is returning your call request."

"It's about time. Kayla, are you all right?" He shouted at the mirror while Nightmare returned to stand at her side.

"I'm fine. Now—"

"How can you be fine, you've been kidnapped." A woman came into view. Her long blonde hair and blue eyes were hauntingly familiar. There was no doubt in her mind this was the woman who'd given birth to her—Raye.

"I was not kidnapped…" Kayla tried to explain, but once again she was cut off.

"Don't be silly, child." Lucian glared at her. "You're in the Shadow Providence, Stormkin terrain. You've been kidnapped. You're a Sunkin. Come home and take your rightful place as Princess." He spoke as if she was a child who didn't know what she was saying.

Impatience threaded through her. "I came here of my own free will."

"But you're a Sunkin Princess." Raye took a step toward the mirror, fluffing her blonde hair.

"I'm a Stormkin Queen. This is my home." As she spoke, Nightmare slid his arm around her. Lucian and Raye watched as their eyes grew as wide as saucers.

"You would allow *them* to touch you?" Lucian asked, each word dripping with hatred and disgust.

She slid her arms around each of her men. "Yes. Now if there's nothing else, we've had a long night."

"You're a Princess—*my* daughter." Raye appeared more stunned than anyone else by Kayla's refusal to travel to the Sunkin land. Her voice cracked as she played with her necklace, seemingly nervous.

"It's nice of you to admit that, Raye. As you told my father, I'm too dark for your tastes. But I'm not a princess, I'm a Queen. A Stormkin Queen." *So suck it.*

"Come here and let your mother see you. Meet the rest of your family before you make your decision," Lucian continued as someone just outside of view handed him a piece of paper.

"I appreciate your offer, Lucian, but I have to decline." She was growing tired of the niceties.

"You will address me as King Lucian." Temper flared in his eyes.

"When you address me by my title, I'll use yours. We are equals, you don't rule over me, and you'll never be *my* King. The misplaced concern for my safety and this illusion of my being kidnapped was touching, but I'm fine…"

"Kayla, I messed up when you were a child…" The hint of regret in Raye's voice didn't touch her expression. "I'm trying to make this right. You're my daughter and I want you to come home."

The woman couldn't lie to her. Kayla could tell she didn't regret her decisions—not one bit.

Dreamer gently rubbed her upper back, calming her.

"Raye, *messed up* is the understatement of the year. You weren't there and you didn't want anything to do with me—*until now*. Now that I've embraced my destiny, all of a sudden you're interested. Nothing has changed between us, because there is no *us*." She nodded to Nightmare; she was done with the call.

Without a word, Kayla slipped away from Dreamer and went to the bed. The last few days had begun to take its toll leaving her both emotionally and physically exhausted. She slipped off her heels and plopped down on the bed. Her evening dress billowed out around her.

"Queen Kayla…" Dreamer came toward her, Nightmare only a step behind.

"Just Kayla, *especially* when we're alone," she told them again, her eyes barely open. When they called her their Queen, it brought all her nagging doubts back to the surface.

"Fine, Kayla—are you all right?" The bed shifted as Nightmare sat next to her.

"Tired." With each second her eyes grew heavier. "Stay with me tonight. I want to feel you both next to me. To know you're safe." From the silence it was clear they were debating it. Nightmare had made it clear he didn't mind sharing her with Dreamer, but he wouldn't physically share her on the same night. "Not sex, I just want you next to me. Both of you."

"Okay. Get ready for bed. I'll contact Shadow Mother and let her know we believe the situation has been resolved with Sunkin King Lucian." Nightmare kissed the top of her head as he stood.

She barely heard him leave, the world drifting around her.

"Come on, doll. You're tired. Let's get you undressed." Dreamer worked the clip and bobby pins out of her hair, letting it free. He stepped away, only to come back seconds later. "I've got a shirt for you. Let's get you out of this dress." He unzipped the back as she did her best to slip out of it without much effort. When it fell to the floor, he slid the shirt over her head. The silky sapphire blue nightshirt laid in deep contrast to her pale skin, coming to rest high on her thigh. Her lingerie always ran on the sexy side; she enjoyed the feel of the cool silk.

She mumbled a thank you. Weeks ago she would have just fallen into bed fully dressed, but now she had Dreamer and Nightmare to look after her.

"Get into bed. We'll change and join you." She all but crawled to the center of the king size bed.

"Lay with me."

"Soon. Nightmare will be back and I'll get out of my suit. Sleep. We'll stay with you."

She wanted to wait until they were both pressed against her, but her body demanded sleep and she lost the battle against it.

Kayla stood in the middle of a forest, fog surrounding her, when someone whispered her name. She stepped forward while the fog moved around her, *with* her. It was unlike anything she'd ever witnessed before; it had a silvery sparkle to it. She wanted to find a way out, but the more she moved the thicker the fog became. Again there was a voice just on the edge of hearing that called her name.

"Who's there?"

No answer. Though the ground was cool under her feet and the wind whipped her hair into her face, something about the place didn't feel real. It was as though she was still in bed between her men, aware she was dreaming. When her name was carried on the wind for the third time, her heart beat a little fast until she saw Dreamer appear just beyond the tree. "What's going on? Where are we?"

"Trust me. I can't keep the connection long." He closed his eyes as if focusing on something.

"Kayla…" Her father's pale figure flickered before her. *What the hell? Did Shadow Mother's Enforcer kill him?* Then he materialized. "I don't have long, but I wanted you to know I'm safe."

"What's going on? Where are we?"

"Dreamer will explain later." He touched her cheek. His touch was solid yet she could still see through him. "I'm sorry about before. I just wanted you safe. Trust Nightmare and Dreamer, they'll protect you while I'm unable. Don't go to the Sunkin land. If you want to meet your mother—which you have every right to—have her go Earthside. Take as many of your trusted guards as you can and go prepared. They'll try whatever they can to get you away from the Stormkins." His figure flickered again. "My time's running out. Be safe. I love you."

Then he was gone and she jerked awake, finding herself sandwiched between a still sleeping Nightmare, and Dreamer who lay awake beside her.

"What was that?" she asked, not expecting an answer.

"I was able to connect your dream with your father. It only lasts for a short time, depending on the distance. He wanted to give you a message."

"He's really safe?" She snuggled into him, still trying to digest what happened.

"Yes. Before I connected your dream to his, he told me he knew this day would come and was prepared. Don't worry about it. You need to focus on you mission for now." He ran his hand down her jawline. "You haven't had time to adjust to this life, but tomorrow we need to start making Storm Hollow a safe haven. Nightmare and I will help you establish laws, and fine-tune your abilities. You need to step into your power now. We can't wait any longer, especially now that Sunkin King Lucian knows you have come home to your people."

# Chapter Twenty-Five

She could hardly sleep. Thoughts of the future preoccupied her. She had kept some of her abilities suppressed, and others would awaken now that she'd returned to the Stormkins. How many more would she have to learn to control? Shooting lightning from her fingertips was challenging enough, she didn't need something just as dangerous. Abilities aside, she had to start thinking about her territory. She had to make it a suitable home for not only her and her men, but also for the half-breeds and unwanted who would soon flock to her land in droves, at least according to Nightmare. They had been outcasts among their own people, and would value a safe haven. But what the hell did she know about any of that?

*Still, a bar is something of a safe haven—or at least it could be. Rules of a bar were a heck of a lot different than defining the law.* "Laws?"

"You'll have to establish your own laws, ones that will protect half-breeds and unwanted Stormkins. That will help deter any issues that can arise from those who still hold prejudices. There needs to be a death sentence to anyone who causes harm to an outcast, when it can be established they did it out of prejudices. Normal duels will be impossible to stop, but challenge duels because of outcast status should be a punishable offense, or Storm Hollow won't become the safe haven we need it to me." Dreamer rubbed her arm.

"Duels?" she questioned uneasily. "Why would anyone challenge someone else to a duel? What's the point?"

Nightmare snuggled against her. "Duels can prove dominance. They can also be used to take over another's position. Many Queens require duels to advance within their Enforcers unit." He gently caressed her thigh.

"That's barbaric...I won't stand for that here. I want it known that anyone who would challenge one of my Enforcers will not earn any favors, they won't be able to use that to advance their position." She reached her hand behind her, running it over his body, gently caressing him.

She laid cuddled in the embrace of her men, content. She wasn't tired, yet she didn't want to leave the comfort of their embrace. She wanted to stay wrapped in their arms, until the warm tentacles of sleep found around them again. She snuggled into Dreamer, using her hand on Nightmare to draw his body tight against her back. The warmth of them surrounding her left her longing for little else.

Her contentment didn't last long. She opened her mouth to say something, but it got lost in the sound of glass breaking as the house shook violently. If she were in California, she would have said it was an earthquake.

Nightmare shot up quickly from the bed, grabbing his handgun from the bedside table. His pale white skin stood out like a painter's canvas against his black shorts in the dim light as he jogged across the room to the door. "Protect our Queen, Dreamer, I'll check it out."

Dreamer rose from the bed, gun in hand. She had a brief moment to wonder where the rest of her Enforcers—Chameleon, Thunder, and Windwalker—were, certain they'd heard the racket.

"Don't move!" Nightmare shouted.

Another blast shook the house, the windows vibrated, and things fell off shelves crashing to the floor. "What the hell was that?"

"They're attacking the house with their magic, trying to break through the protection, but it's resilient because I reinforced it earlier to make certain no one with ill intent could get in." A breeze picked up out of nowhere as Dreamer looked toward the window.

When she stood he pulled her close to him, his gun raised, but not aimed at anything in particular, since there was nothing to shoot at—at least nothing she could see. The wind inside the room picked up, blowing her hair into her face as Dreamer pushed her behind him.

Air was sucked from her lungs, leaving her slightly dizzy. A figure appeared, blurred by the mist of the wind, and approached. Dreamer raised his gun, lining his sight on the viable target.

Windwalker appeared, his long white hair reminding her of freshly fallen snow as it blew behind him like a cape. "Don't shoot." He held his hands out, showing he was unarmed, despite the long steel blade strapped across his back.

"Damn it, Windwalker. What the hell were you thinking? We could have shot you." Dreamer lowered his gun to his waist, but didn't put it away.

"If there was another way I would have done it. But to protect my Queen I would risk my life."

The wind ended as quickly as it began, leaving her hair to fall around her again. She pushed it out of her face, watching the men. "What's going on, Windwalker?"

"Chameleon and Thunder are moving in to assist Nightmare. I came to warn you to stay here with Dreamer, we can't have you running off and getting injured on your second night in Storm Hollow." He headed to the door, drawing his sword.

"Do you know who's attacking?"

"Blake and River." With that he left, and silence hung heavily in the air.

"Who are they?" *Not sure what's worse, the people I have to interview or the ones who want to kill me.*

"They're brothers, and they've been in hiding for years. Blake used to be Queen Shower's right hand man, until she denied him a place in her bed. None of us were sure what happened to get him tossed aside." Dreamer grabbed a t-shirt that lay discarded at the bottom of the bed. "He's unstable, making him dangerous, and his ability to snuff out the light makes him even more so. River's abilities only work if he's around a river, hence his namesake. He can call a river to him, drowning his enemy."

He pivoted and went to the window.

The rigidity in his posture worried her. "You thought of something. What is it?"

"I've never seen only two of them—they're triplets like us—so I'm wondering where Wind is."

"Another 'Wind'?" Did no one have a name that wasn't their ability? Was there some ceremony where they received an honorific name? She went to stand next to him and looked out over the grounds. A few lights were on in the town as people went about their normal lives and prepared themselves for the day ahead.

"My Queen, get away from the window. Everyone always forgets about the windows. You feel safe and secure inside the house, while someone is just waiting for you to walk past. We might be immortal but a bullet wound is painful and I don't want to see you go through that."

*Immortal?* Reluctantly, she obeyed. His job was to keep her safe and she had to let him do it. She still couldn't wrap her mind around the fact that she was immortal. She would never grow old, at least not in the way humans did. *When this is all over I'll have to ask more about this immortality.*

"Come over here." He pulled her into the sitting area and flipped on the laptop. "This will allow us to tap into the security and see what's going on."

"You check. It's chilly, I'm going to get some pants." She pulled away and went to the closet, her thoughts turning to Nightmare. *Is he safe? I don't know what I'll do if something happens to him.* She tried to listen to see if she could hear anything, any sign of him.

*God is this what my life has really become?* She grabbed a pair of pants and dragged them on hurriedly.

The bedroom doors being kicked out of the frame caused her to spin around. *What the hell?* The door landed with a thump against the hardwood floor. It only took her a moment to realize the intruder hadn't kicked in the doors; he'd blown them open. It was Wind.

"Queen, come with me and I'll let Dreamer live. Or he can join your other men in the afterlife, and you'll still come with me, but you'll suffer as well." Wind stepped over the door, a smaller man following, his gun drawn.

Dreamer said something but all she could think was, *Dead? Nightmare can't be dead.*

"I don't know what Blake told you, but there's no reason for you to be here." Dreamer's tone was calm, but his gun was raised as he tried to make his way to her.

"She'll be the end of us, of all the Stormkins. I won't die for some half-breed bitch. It's despicable that Shadow Mother thinks she's on our side." He pushed his hand forward and shoved Dreamer back with a harsh blast of wind.

"Wind, look at me," she commanded, drawing his attention. His cold, hard eyes were full of darkness. "I'm not here to hurt anyone. Whatever's happened, let me help you." She focused on her anger and her grief, to have it ready if she needed to call her lightning.

"Bitch, do you really think I'm going to fall for that?" His rage sent another harsh gust of wind at them. She braced herself for it, but Dreamer was closer and took the brunt of it. He landed hard, but his aim was steady. He opened fire and bullets slammed into Wind, but that didn't stop him. She held her ground. If her journey ended here, then she would go down fighting.

Wind shot another gale toward Dreamer, sending him crashing into the wall on the far side of the room.

She didn't have time to worry about Dreamer, she had her own problem headed straight for her—Wind himself. She searched for something to use as a weapon, but nothing was reachable. Clothes, shoes, nothing she could use to defend herself. Dreamer was trying to fight off another intruder, a smaller man, leaving her to handle Wind. She raised her arms, holding out her hands to keep him away, trying to focus on pushing her anger through her fingers. Her lightning might be her only savior, if Dreamer couldn't escape to help her in time. Out of the corner of her eye she saw him drop the limp man. With one problem eliminated he was coming toward her, but it was going to be too late because Wind was nearly upon her.

The smaller man Dreamer dropped limply to the floor only moments before was now a pile of ash. She didn't have time to wonder. She looked at Dreamer one last time, burning the image into her mind; if she was going to die, she wanted him to be the last thing she saw.

Heat washed over her, warming her skin. The warmth traveled down her arm like fire blazing through her and then it burst from her hand. Gray flames licked her fingertips, a split second before an immense splintering of deep blue and gray flames hit Wind in the chest. The fire coated his skin and Wind screamed.

*What the hell have I done?*

Dreamer raced around the flaming Wind, careful to stay out of the direct line of her hands, and took position next to her.

She stood there watching unable to tear herself away, her stomach lurching. His screams died as quickly as they began as if someone had flicked the switch to turn off the sound. His body disintegrated into a pile of ash.

Sickened, she collapsed, unable to reconcile her soul with her actions.

She'd taken a man's life in self-defense, killed him with magic. Did that make her heartless? Maybe, but all she could feel was relief.

"Kayla, answer me." Anxiety coated Dreamer's words.

She turned her head to find him inches from her, his breath hot on her skin, his forehead creased with worry. Had he been calling her all this time? Strange, she hadn't heard him. "What?"

"Are you okay?"

"I'm fine." She stared down at her hands, the heat replaced by a chill wrapping around her body. "What did I do?"

"You called fire." He pulled her to her feet.

"How? I shoot lightning not flames. How did this happen?"

She couldn't tear her gaze from the pile of ashes in the center of the room.

# Chapter Twenty-Six

Kayla curled up on the bed, her legs drawn close to her chest. The chill clung to her body. The voices of her men dominated the space, but for the life of her, she didn't know what they said. She heard the words, but couldn't make sense of them.

The mattress depressed next to her, forcing her to look away from the spot on the rug. Turning her head away slowly, as if something bad would happen if she looked away from the rug, she found Nightmare sitting next to her. For the first time she could read the concern on his face clearly.

"My Queen." He wrapped his large hands around hers, drawing them into his lap. "This newest ability will make others fear you more."

"But how…I don't understand. How is any of this possible? I thought my ability was lightning."

"I told you, most Queens have multiple abilities. There will be more."

Would her other abilities be worse than what she had just done? She stared back at the ashes.

"Besides bringing to life my fears, can you do anything else?" Focusing on his hands, she regained the reality she'd lost. Out of the corner of her gaze she could see Dreamer sitting on the edge of the bed, watching them.

Nightmare nodded. "During a fight, I can pull the energy from my opponent and make it my own. I can also heal, but not in the way of most healers."

"Heal? What does that mean?" She couldn't help but wonder why her own abilities had to cause destruction instead of healing.

Nightmare ran his thumb across the back of her hand, his gaze on her while his thoughts seemed to be elsewhere.

As if Dreamer realized Nightmare wouldn't answer, he rose, and came toward her. She couldn't take her eyes off the way his body moved, the dim light cascading off his toned abs. "That doesn't matter now. The fire...it's not a Stormkin ability. I believe you get the ability from your mixed heritage, but you're Stormkin half has made it darker, turning the flames deep blue and gray."

She tried not to care; after all the fire had saved her life. She had no time for regret, or second-guessing her abilities if she wanted to survive. "Will I have others caused by my Sunkin side?"

Dreamer hesitated before answering. "It's possible."

"No matter how it came, it saved your life tonight." Nightmare's fingers slid between hers, joining their hands together as one. "You need to get some sleep."

Her gaze skirted the room, to once again fall on the pile of ashes near the closet. "Later." Even to her own ears, her voice sounded tired, and lifeless. Slipping her hand out of his, she rose, determined to clean the mess she had created.

Nightmare wrapped his large hand around her wrist, not letting her go. "Your storm elf, Raven, will attend to it. Let Dreamer and I attend to you."

"I can't lay feet away from..." She started to say it, but *it* had been a person.

"We'll go to another room. Raven will gather the ashes and return them to his family."

"The other brothers…" She feared she knew the answer, but had to ask. She had to hear him say it to know it was true.

"They've been eliminated. Thunder's on his way to contact the surviving family. Come, let Dreamer and I hold you. In the morning we'll deal with the damage, with everything."

Not waiting for her answer, he swept her into his arms.

She knew it was morning by looking at the numbers that glared at her from the bedside table. She hadn't slept. She laid snug against Nightmare's body, her leg draped over him holding him closer, while Dreamer curled around the back of her, his hand resting on her thigh. Her men kept her grounded in the here and now instead of thinking about what happened hours before in the other room.

"My Queen, you're to meet Gideon this morning. Do you want me to reschedule it?" Dreamer's fingers traced along her hip, down her thigh.

"No. I'll see him. It's not good to lay around doing nothing."

"If you're worried about doing nothing, I think we can fix that." Nightmare laid a soft kiss on her forehead.

"I'm sure we could, but we need to build a strong group of Enforcers. Windwalker, Chameleon, Thunder, and Storm, are not enough guards. I'm supposed to meet with Mist as well."

"Mist will be a good Enforcer, but I wouldn't entrust your safety to him until he has some training under him. If you wish to promote him to Enforcer he'll start by guarding the grounds." He ran his hand along her arm. "By the next council meeting, I'd like you to have at least ten elite Enforcers for your protection."

"If Gideon works out, then we'll have five besides you two." She ran one hand over Nightmare's bare chest, while she took hold of Dreamer's hand with her other hand. "Thank you."

"For what?" Dreamer asked.

"For last night, staying with me, holding me. For just being you."

"It was our pleasure." Dreamer kissed her cheek. "I'll get your clothes from the other room." He rose, leaving her alone with Nightmare, neither of them ready to rise.

"I want to promote Dreamer to Lieutenant Enforcer." Nightmare propped himself up on his elbow to look down at her. Even in bed, half-naked, he was all business. "He'll be my second in command, if something happens to me he'll make sure you're safe. He'll also be in charge of the Enforcers' training, schedules for the ground Enforcers, recruiting for the training course. His main priority will still be your protection, and this will give him more responsibility, help him develop his own authority, so he's not just an Enforcer under my command."

"Then do it." She leaned up on her elbow and stared down at him.

"This is your territory, it should be your decision."

"I trust both of you with my life. I made you my Enforcer in Charge because I knew you would make sure I was safe in this new world. Dreamer is the same way but he looks to you for approval. This will give him the chance he needs to stand on his own two feet, to gain confidence."

"After over seven hundred years, you'd think he would have the confidence."

"Seven hundred?" She gaped. *Did he just say seven hundred? He's over seven hundred years old?*

"Yes. I told you we're immortal." His cupid bow lips curled up in a half smile.

"Immortal yes, but you didn't mention you were that—"

"Old? Why, does it bother you?"

"No. I figured you've been around longer than I could have guessed. You were in the war with my father, which means you had to be at least as old as him, if not older, but I never thought of your age. It did come to my attention that sometimes when you speak it's very formal, as if you're from another time. Well I guess you are…" She realized she was rambling but she couldn't believe her lovers were over seven hundred.

"Your father is older…by at least two hundred years."

Sitting up, she wrapped her arms around her knees as sadness tightened her chest.

"What's wrong? Are you worried about your father?" He brushed her back and she tensed at the contact.

"I just can't wrap my head around this immortality business…I mean, I've aged. Are you sure I'm immortal? Maybe I'm not because of my mixed heritage, or because I was born and raised Earthside. Maybe I'm just a ship in the sea that is your life. I won't be around for centuries like the rest of you."

"You're immortal, I'm sure of it. We stop aging once we come into our powers. Now that you're home with us and your powers have developed, it'll be the same for you. There are very few ways to kill us. You've never really been human even though you've lived among them. You'd have aged if you'd stayed there, but you'd never age like the average human. You're a Stormkin."

Dreamer opened the door and stepped into the room before she could come up with something to say. Not that she knew what she would say anyway.

# Chapter Twenty-Seven

Kayla sat once again in the long conference room, leaning back against the stiff leather chair as she watched the man across from her. His hair was a reddish shade that reminded her of rust with auburn highlights throughout. He surveyed her with his smoky gray eyes as if he waiting for an attack; only briefly did his gaze flash to the men at her back.

Nightmare and Dreamer flanked her on either side, waiting for her. They would take her lead as she interviewed Gideon. Even with her own mixed heritage, she wasn't convinced having another with Sunkin genes would be as beneficial as Nightmare believed. Concern that he'd betray her and her men teased along her thoughts.

"Queen Kayla, I've traveled far to see you. I left my homeland some time ago, but I would give much to find a true place among my own people again. What do you require of me?" His voice held a deep longing she couldn't ignore.

"Gideon, do you honestly consider the Stormkins your people? Or do you hold some grudge against us because you are of mixed blood?"

"I'm no more mixed blood than you, my Queen. Do you hold a grudge against the Stormkins?"

"Gideon…" Dreamer growled behind her.

"It's fine, Dreamer." She watched Gideon for a moment. "Point taken, but I wasn't raised around the Sunkins for part of my life. You were raised by them, so you can see my concern."

"You've done your research." His gaze flickered to Nightmare. "Though that was hundreds of years ago and only for a short time. I've been raised here most of my life, with my father, and his beliefs ingrained into me. I was never truly welcomed in the land of the sun, not as I've been here. I consider myself a Stormkin."

"What are your abilities?" She twirled the ring on her finger, watching him.

"Fire…I can manifest fire in my hand, but I'm also a firebreather." He tipped his head back, staring at the ceiling as he let out a breath. Short blue and green flames sprouted out of his open mouth. When he closed his mouth, the flames disappeared, and he turned back to her. "My father could shift into a dragon."

"Interesting talent." She leaned forward, putting her hands on top of the table. "You left after your father's death. Why do you now want to come back, to give up the freedom you've found?"

"Shadow Providence, especially Storm Hollow, has always been my home. I don't fit Earthside. I left because I'd have been killed under Queen Shower. She saw my mixed blood as the ultimate sin. I stood no chance against her. The only protection I had from her wrath was my father. She would have lost his protection…his company in her bed." His gaze fell to the table as if embarrassed by the last part.

"Return Earthside, tie up loose ends, gather your belongings, and report within forty-eight hours. When you report be prepared to pledge your allegiance to me. If you can't do that, don't return."

He pushed back his chair and rose. "Yes, my Queen. I'll return promptly. Thank you."

When the door clicked shut, she sighed.

"Is everything all right?" Dreamer laid his hand on her shoulder.

"Just tired. I..." Her words were cut off by a knock on the door, seconds before Chameleon entered, Storm on his heels.

Sword drawn, Chameleon bowed his head to her, but wasted no time on pleasantries. "Nightmare, you're needed. There's an issue downstairs, Windwalker has someone detained."

"Dreamer, take the Queen back to her room." His hand brushed against her arm, before he turned back to the other men. "You two go with them. Where's Thunder?"

"With Windwalker."

"Very well. Now go." Nightmare left without waiting to see if they followed orders.

Dreamer took hold of her arm and pulled her to her feet in a fluid motion. Together with Storm and Chameleon, they escorted her to the private suite. Where she might have questioned their suspicion before, the attack the previous night reminded her they couldn't be paranoid enough.

"Chameleon, who's downstairs? Maybe it's Breezy, she's supposed to join me for lunch."

"It's not Breezy. Inside your room." Chameleon nudged her inside and they secured the door.

"Who is it?" When no one answered she looked to each of the men. "Damn it, someone answer me. I am your Queen, you must answer a direct question. Chameleon, who did you see downstairs?"

"Darkness."

Dreamer's hand tensed on her arm with Chameleon's statement. *Who the hell is Darkness?* "Dreamer, what is it? Who is this Darkness?"

"Chameleon, go assist them. Storm and I will stay with the Queen,"

Dreamer ordered.

When Chameleon didn't step away from the door she raised an eyebrow at him. "You were given an order."

"My Queen, you need all the guards you can with you."

"Chameleon, I don't know who Darkness is, but if Dreamer feels that assisting Nightmare and the others is more important than staying here, take it as a direct order from me. Now go!"

"As my Queen wishes." He bowed his head, and hurried back out the door. Storm locked it behind him.

"Dreamer, tell me who this Darkness is."

"If a Queen needed someone eliminated they call him. He's an assassin."

*Assassin…here for me?*

"We'll keep you safe at all costs."

There would be costs. She'd already seen that.

Minutes passed like hours while Kayla waited for Nightmare to return to her. As her Enforcer in Charge, his reality would be one of constant risk—but she couldn't picture herself in this strange world without him and Dreamer.

Dreamer sat with her, one arm around her, but his attention was focused elsewhere. She wanted to take comfort in his nearness, but everything seemed to ride on a knife's edge.

Footsteps came down the hall outside; seconds later the door handle jingled. Dreamer shot to his feet, shielding her with his body.

"It's Nightmare."

The sound of his voice relaxed him. She stood, but Dreamer wouldn't let her go around him. In a few quick strides Storm reached the door, unlocking it to admit Nightmare.

Satisfied it was safe, Dreamer stepped to the side to let her pass.

"Nightmare." Her voice softened and she hurried over to embrace him. "You're okay."

"I'm fine." He wrapped his arms tightly around her. "Storm, stand outside the door. I need to speak with our Queen alone." Storm stepped out immediately.

"What does Darkness want? Is he here to kill me?"

Nightmare shot Dreamer a quick look before lowering her to the sofa and taking a seat beside her. "Dreamer told you who he is then. No, he's not here for you, at least not in the way you expect." He turned sideways, to look at her. "He says he's grown tired of his life, always being at the beck and call of different Queens. He has sought a ruler for years, but no one would allow him in their territory, at least not permanently. He has come to seek a place in Storm Hollow, with you as his Queen."

"No." The resentment was clear in Dreamer's voice. "He's a killer."

"We all have blood on our hands." Nightmare eyed Dreamer as if there was some other issue boiling under the surface. Dreamer despised Darkness.

"Storm said he kills half-breeds. Why would he want to serve under me?"

"He's only killed when ordered. He's an assassin. His father was an assassin and so is he. There's very little change in our community, a parent's jobs passes to their children. It keeps the balance. He's never killed for sport."

He told her that over the centuries he had to develop a tone that hid his emotions, or risk the wrath of his ruler. Even with her, where he didn't have to fear her, his tone was always natural. For the first time since he'd walked into her bar, she caught the first betrayal of that tone. There was a hint of distrust and anxiety hidden behind that perfect mask. "But you don't trust him."

He didn't answer for a long time, just stared across the short space at her. Emotions passed in his green eyes too fast for her to take them in. "I don't. I don't believe he's here to kill you, but I'm not sure I believe his excuse of being tired of his life. If that was the case he could have quit accepting jobs. He's one of the few Stormkins who has a house outside of our lands. He could go there. To have him come here so soon after your arrival in our land draws questions."

"Then send him away."

"If I may…granted Darkness is a risk, but if you use your gift you'll be able to see his true objective. He would be a great ally if his intentions are true."

Dreamer pushed from the sofa and marched across the room to stand next to the window. It was clear he hated the idea and more than anything she wanted to know why. What had Darkness cost him?

Unable to tear her gaze from Dreamer, she nodded and told Nightmare, "Take him to the conference room. Dreamer will escort me there shortly."

# Chapter Twenty-Eight

Silence blanketed the room in Nightmare's absence. She studied Dreamer for a long time before approaching him. His anger circled him like electricity, crackling and burning the air.

She leaned against the wall, out of direct line of sight to the window. "Tell me."

"There's nothing to tell." He was lying; his body language was closed off and practically screamed *don't touch*. "If you wish to accept Darkness into your territory it's fine, for I have no say."

"Dreamer, your opinion matters to me as much as Nightmare's. Now what's between you and Darkness? Why can't you even say his name without hatred dripping from each syllable? Tell me what's going on here." She grabbed hold of his arm, demanding he look at her. He could have stopped her, but instead he met her mid-motion, sadness in his eyes.

"Our mother's sister—Aunt D—she was unstable, for as long as I can remember. Her true abilities never manifested, they lay under the surface, causing her pain until her mind broke. I would help Mom look after Aunt D, try to keep her hidden from others. One night while everyone slept, she went into town and caused quite a stir. Enforcers brought her home, but it was too late. Queen Shower found out, she determined her unfit and Darkness was brought in." His voice was cold, distant.

"I'm sorry, Dreamer." She slipped her around his back, drawing her body close to him.

"What Nightmare didn't tell you is Darkness is the reason for our mother's death. She tried to protect her sister. We lost both of them that night."

She didn't know what to say. No words could express the sorrow she had for him. This was years ago, yet to Dreamer the wounds were fresh. Having Darkness serve as a constant reminder of the death of his family would only serve to push Dreamer deeper into the shell she was finally beginning to get him out of.

"I'm sorry, love." She pressed her body tighter to him. Minutes passed, his muscles uncoiled, relaxed, but she continued to hold him until she was satisfied he was okay. "I have to see him. If you wish to wait here for me or outside the conference room doors, I'll understand."

"You're my Queen. I'll be by your side in all things."

She leaned in close, kissed him gently. He tasted of the air after a summer storm. She couldn't get enough. She pressed a hand to his chest. The urge to push him onto the bed was overwhelming, but others waited on her. She'd have to put her hormones on the back burner until later.

"Let's get this over with."

She spent more time in the conference room than anywhere else and she was truly beginning to hate the gray walls and the long mahogany table. The man sitting across the table watched her carefully. His eyes guarded, taking her in as if she was a piece of meat.

She looked him over, studying him as he studied her. His midnight black hair stood out in comparison to his creamy pale skin. His lips set in a stern line. She realized he was trying to intimidate her, but it didn't work. Instead, his dark black eyes sparkled as if stars were scattered across them.

"My Queen." Nightmare pulled out a chair for her.

"Thank you." She sat, still watching Darkness, but no longer looking in his eyes. "Darkness, why have you come?"

There was a faint trace of amusement in his eyes. "Straight to the point is unusual in a Queen."

"I've never been one to beat around the bush, and I don't have time to be any other way. Now get to the point of this unannounced visit or this meeting is over and you can leave." She could feel the presence of both of her men behind her, tense and waiting for Darkness to step out of line. More guards waited outside the door, ready to pounce if there was even a hint of the strangest noise from inside the room.

His gaze flashed from her to Dreamer, then to Nightmare before returning. "I've come to seek a proper place in your territory."

"Why?"

"I'm assuming *they* told you what I do." There was a deep animosity in his voice when he said *they*.

She nodded once, motioning for him to get on with it.

"I had no choice but to go into this life. It was my father's profession, as it was his father's as well. I never wanted to be an assassin. I'm well over five hundred and have taken more lives than I care to say. I don't want to do it any longer, but unless I find a Queen who will grant me a place in her land I'm stuck."

He sounded truthful, but if she was going to risk having an assassin who could possibly be trading information to her enemies she needed more proof than just his word. She required solid proof. "I'm aware you own a house outside of our lands. You could go there."

"I do. I spend my time there between assignments, but this is my home.

I won't wither and die for lack of my homeland, but it's like being lost at sea surrounded by water yet unable to quench your thirst."

"I can't allow…" Even as she spoke, he started to rise and her men reach for their weapons. "Darkness, what do you think you're doing?"

"Leaving. That's what you want, isn't it? You were going to say you can't allow me here." He stood between the table and chair, waiting for her to speak. "It's what they all say."

He was shorter than she expected. His wide frame of toned muscles was barely six foot. She had expected his large chest to have equally long legs to go with it.

She frowned. "If this is how you treat a Queen, I can see why no one wants you in their territory. Now sit down and hear me out before you go running off with your tail between your legs."

"I apologize, Queen Kayla." He sat, his gaze not meeting hers.

"That's the first time you've addressed me properly."

"It's been a long time since I've dealt directly with royalty, I've forgotten my manners. I apologize again, Queen Kayla."

She nodded, not entirely convinced. "Very well. Now as I was saying…I can't allow you to remain in Storm Hollow unless I have proof that what you say is the truth. That there isn't a hidden plot behind your words."

"How do you expect me to prove it to you?"

"You won't have to do anything. Just give me your hand." She placed her hands on the table, reaching across to him.

"What will this do?" He held his hand hesitantly above the table near him.

"It won't hurt, it'll allow me to know what your true plans are. If you have ulterior motives I suggest you leave now because my Enforcers will not stand for a betrayal."

He slid his hand across the table, surprisingly timid despite his reputation.

Wrapping her hands around his she brought the connection to life. She closed her eyes, focusing on what she needed to know. She didn't want to see the missions he had gone on, the people he had murdered. She sought out his reason for coming to Storm Hollow, and then she had another goal in mind.

She saw a vision of Darkness with a man who could have been his twin if he wasn't older, his hair lighter. They were arguing, both furious.

*You're my son and I'll be damned if I'll have you disgrace me. You'll take your place as an assassin or you'll leave Shadow Providence like your brother did. You saw what happened to him, do you really want to follow in his footsteps? Now grab your weapons, today you'll complete your first mission. I won't have your mother sheltering you from your destiny any longer. Let's go.*

The young Darkness followed his father, sword in hand, his shoulders sunk in defeat.

She watched his life unfold before her eyes, skipping the missions and anything that didn't affect what was happening today. She felt like a voyeur, and considered breaking the bond until the she recognized Nightmare in one of the memories. She stopped and tried to focus on it. The fact Darkness fought her bond only made her pry deeper into the memory.

*She meant no harm. Please...* The woman begged, tears running down her face, her light brown hair spilling around her as she ran toward the other woman cowering on the ground. Nightmare was off to the side, engaged in battle with Darkness's father.

*"Kill her, son, or the Queen will demand your death for disobedience,"* the man shouted. Darkness held his sword inches from the woman who appeared to be Aunt D; he could have taken the killing shot then, but he'd hesitated,

giving the other woman time to reach them. She pulled Aunt D to her feet, and shielded her with her body.

*"She's harmless, there's no reason for anyone to fear my sister. Please, take me to the Queen, I'll explain it to her. There's no reason for this,"* the woman begged.

Darkness looked to his father, shaking his head. *"Enough,"* he called. *"We'll take them to the Queen. If death is ordered then it's my head, not yours, Father."*

Nightmare swung his sword around, ready to defend himself against both, but the older man slipped away and rushed the women with deadly speed. Both had been killed before he could react. His mother and aunt, slain in a heartbeat.

Nightmare stared down at the bodies of the two women he cared about and something snapped inside of him. She could see a wildness in his eyes as he drove his sword straight through Darkness's father, before pulling it out, doing it again and again, chopping at his body like a crazed killer until there was nothing left but a pile of meat that had once been a person.

She realized her Dreamer carried a grudge against a man for decades when it wasn't his fault. He had to know the truth, see what really happened that day, but first she had to speak with her men alone. She slipped her hand from his, breaking the connection, and sank back into her chair exhausted.

"Wait in the hall." She felt hollow, as though all the life had been drained from her body.

"Yes, Queen Kayla." Darkness rose, appearing almost as exhausted as she felt.

# Chapter Twenty-Nine

Her ability to see someone's memories had never fatigued her this much in the past. She felt as if she'd been running, her body aching all over. She took a moment to gather her strength before swinging her chair around to her men.

"Dreamer, wait outside, I need to have a moment with our Queen." Nightmare nodded to the door. It wasn't until Dreamer shut it behind him that Nightmare continued. "You saw what happened, didn't you?"

She could have said no and let him tell his side, but she didn't. She was tired, and wanted to get to the bottom of it before Breezy arrived for lunch. "Yes. You have to tell Dreamer what happened. He has to know it wasn't Darkness who killed them, or he'll never move past it. Why didn't you tell him the truth?"

"Queen Shower would have ordered my death if any word of what truly occurred got back to her. They weren't there to kill me…our customs say the only one who can defend himself is the one who's sentenced to death. Unless it's a ruler, then the Enforcers step in. Otherwise if you kill the assassin, the Queen can order your death for the loss of the assassin. There are very few assassins among us now, as most Queens prefer to do their own dirty work, or have their Enforcers carry out the punishments. But it was the way for centuries."

"Now?"

"After all these years...I didn't know he still held the grudge, I thought he forgot about it after all this time. It wasn't until today I realized..."

Her neck hurt from looking up at him, she rose to meet him eye to eye. "Knowing he was here, but not knowing why, opened up old wounds. We weren't sure if he was here to kill me."

"I'd never allow that." He reached for her hand. "You're my Queen. I'll protect you with my life."

"I know." *That's the part that bothers me...I don't want to be here without you and Dreamer next to me.* She squeezed his hand. "I can show him what happened, but he needs to hear it from you."

He nodded. "I know." He let her hand fall from his and walked to the door. "Dreamer."

She strolled to the window, giving them what privacy she could. She wrapped her arms around her body, trying to shake the chill that settled into her bones after she'd broken the connection. She watched outside the window, wondering what she was going to do about Darkness, when Dreamer touched her shoulder.

"I apologize, I didn't mean to startle you."

"It's okay, Dreamer, I was lost in thought. You okay?" She slipped her arm around his waist, underneath his suit jacket.

"Nightmare said you can show me what happened. I need to see it."

"Okay." She pressed herself against his toned body, her head resting against his chest. Just holding him close to her, feeling his warmth and security, helped her relax. "Darkness is being truthful; he never wanted the life he was born into."

"He's dangerous." Dreamer rubbed her back. "Putting aside my feelings I know he would be a powerful ally, but he's also dangerous."

"If he's on our side, the danger is working for us," Nightmare stated, making it clear it was better to have the assassin *with* them rather than *against* them.

"I don't think he's a danger to us. Otherwise I wouldn't have him here. When bringing in powerful allies, I want to make sure they are completely on our side. I'd rather them out of my territory, than have to watch over my shoulder and have them here." Raising her arm, she held her hand out to Nightmare, craving his touch as well of Dreamer's.

Dreamer seemed to be considering all the options. "Having him here in Storm Hollow will make your enemies hesitate."

"To make them hesitate you need to make him one of your Enforcers. If others see him guarding you, they know what he's capable of, and they'll stay back." Nightmare took her hand and slipped his other arm around her waist, below Dreamer's. "My Queen, if I may…if you're comfortable with what you saw, I'd suggest you accept him into your land. If he pledges his allegiance to you, he's bound to you. If he goes against you in any way you can exile him or demand his death. If you're worried about him and your safety, don't be, we'll protect you."

"I know. I'm just concerned about everything. He must have his own enemies."

"Yes, I'm positive he has enemies, but they're not stupid enough to attack an Enforcer, especially one that spent years as an assassin. You need to consider the benefits over the risks."

She stayed sandwiched between her men, debating her options. Could Dreamer really handle Darkness being a permanent member of their team?

"Bring him in."

Nightmare pressed a soft kiss to her check. "I think you're doing the right thing."

She tilted her head, looking up at Dreamer. "Are you okay with this?"

"Your safety means more to me than my grudge. He'll make some hesitate and will stop other potential attacks." He lowered his head, leaning close to her. "Don't worry about me. I'm fine as long as I have you by my side." He kissed her. It ended too quickly for her, but the door opened and Nightmare and Darkness re-entered.

"Darkness, take a seat." She stepped out of Dreamer's embrace but kept her hand in his, taking him with her as she walked across the room. "Your memory about Nightmare and Dreamer's mother...I need to show it to Dreamer. I could do it myself but I feel that you should be a part of this."

Darkness's gaze shot to Nightmare before turning back to her. "Darkness, I'm Queen here, not Nightmare. We know why you two never told anyone what happened that day, but Dreamer needs to know. Queen Shower is dead, she can't punish you or any of us for that day."

"Shadow Mother can." His hesitation echoed in the words. It seemed even he feared Shadow Mother.

"No one outside this room will know. Dreamer deserves to know what happened to his mother and aunt." She lowered herself in the chair she vacated earlier, and laid her hand on the table. "Either you do this or you can leave now. There's no second chances. It's now or never. Once Dreamer sees what he needs to we can discuss a potential place in Storm Hollow. If you choose not to help me, I'll still show him, and you will leave this place, never to return." She made sure he knew Dreamer would know what happened either way. The power might be new to her but she was aware there was another way to show Dreamer the truth *without* being the connecting rod so he could see it straight from Darkness.

He hesitated only a moment longer before slipping his hand into hers. She firmed her hold on Dreamer and let the connection flow through her into Dreamer Leaning back in her chair she watched the memory unfold again before her eyes. This time it drained the remaining energy she had from her body, making her feel as though she floated through the air.

When it finished she quickly pulled her hands back, breaking the connection, her breath coming in short gasps. Fatigue swamped her.

"My Queen, are you okay?" Nightmare knelt beside her, and touched her thigh.

"I'm fine." Each syllable required a hell of a lot more effort. "Darkness, if you wish to pledge your commitment to me be back here at two o'clock this afternoon. Go tie up whatever lose ends you might have."

"Yes, my Queen. Thank you for this opportunity," he told her as he rose from the table.

"Know this, Darkness, I'll be watching you. If you betray me, step one foot out of bounds, I'll see the punishment fits the crime, and if your life is the cost so be it. I won't have a traitor in my land."

"I only wish to serve you. I mean no harm to you or anyone in your territory. I know the prophecy about you. You'll make this land what it once was. No matter the cost, I'll give whatever assistance I can to see you accomplish this. May I ask what my position will be in your land?"

Nightmare rose, answering his question. "You'll be an Enforcer. As Enforcer in Charge you'll report to me and until I'm satisfied you will not guard our Queen alone. There will be at least one other guard with you at all times. This is a precaution to keep her safe."

Darkness nodded. "I understand. If I were in your place, I wouldn't trust her safety to someone with my past. I hope in time I'll be able to prove myself to you."

"Then go, attend to what you need to and report back here on time. Our Queen needs to rest, her ability has exhausted her." Not watching to see if

Darkness followed his orders, Nightmare lowered himself beside her again, kneeling next to her as he scooped her hand in his much larger one. "Kayla, you should rest for a while."

"In a bit, I'm too tired to move. I'll just sit here for a while." She let her head fall back against the soft leather of the chair, her eyes once again drifting shut.

"Dreamer, make sure Darkness leaves the premises and then meet us in her bedroom." He slid his arm under her legs, and the other one behind her back.

Her eyes shot open, glaring at him. "What do you think you're doing?"

"I'm carrying you to your room." He stood with her in his arms as if she weighed nothing.

"No way, it's out of the question. If I'm going anywhere I'll walk. Now put me down."

"Be sensible. You're exhausted, I won't allow you to waste precious energy. We need you at your best, tonight you have to address your people. Half-breed Stormkins will be flocking here after your announcement, so we must be prepared." He walked to the door that Dreamer had left slightly ajar, and used his foot to kick it open. "Windwalker, Chameleon, with me. Thunder, you're off duty until tonight. Storm, I want you downstairs, no one's admitted until Breezy arrives to see the Queen. Also tell Raven to serve lunch in the Queen's private sitting room. Escort Breezy there when she arrives."

With no alternative, she rested her head against his chest. She might have fought them if they were alone, but in front of the other Enforcers it would make her appear weaker than she already did. If anyone thought Nightmare ruled her kingdom instead of her they would probably use that as an excuse to see her executed. It would also lead to the death of Nightmare and Dreamer as they had decimated the only door that remained open to them when they left Shadow Mother's service. No, she had to stay alive if not for herself but for the people who counted on her.

She relaxed into his embrace. His rock hard chest was cool against her flushed face. His strong arms supported her, making her feel safe and secure in his grasp. He was one of the greatest warriors of all Stormkins, and men followed him without question. It was an advantage to have him by her side, instead of against her. Even with the power and command he held over the Enforcers, she would've had him by her side regardless. After all, she loved him.

# Chapter Thirty

"My Queen, if you're ready, Breezy is here." Dreamer strolled into her bedroom looking as if he'd just stepped out of a photo shoot. He was happier than she'd ever seen him; the glow around him proved it. As much as he and Nightmare sheltered their younger half-sister, they loved and missed her. She hesitated to think of the consequences if their enemies ever learned of their connection. Breezy could be used like a pawn in a large game of chess.

"Come here, Dreamer." Desire laced her voice.

He closed the distance between them in two short strides. When he stopped in front of her, she raised her arms, running her hands along his crisp white dress shirt until she could slip her arm around his neck. "Are you truly okay with Darkness's presence in Storm Hollow, having him as an Enforcer here?"

"This is your kingdom, I'm only your Enforcer so I have no say." His gaze locked onto hers, the deep green sparkled; even the mention of Darkness didn't take his happiness away as it had before.

"Your opinion matters to me."

"I know the truth about what happened and I'm moving past it. But it doesn't change the fact he's been an assassin for over five hundred years. It's hard to change, especially when it's been ingrained in you for so long. The boy who was there the day my family was killed is different from the man who stood before you today. He's harder now, colder, there's no sympathy left in him."

"We all have blood on our hands. Still, we make a good team." She tried to make light of Darkness's past, even though the amount of blood he'd spilt bothered her as well.

"You killed in self-defense," he reminded her. "Nightmare and I have done it in battle, duels, and at our Queen's orders, but never as Darkness has done it." He slipped his arm higher up her back. "I want you safe."

"You and Nightmare will keep me safe. Nightmare already told him he wouldn't be guarding me without one of you." She rose to her tippy toes to kiss him. Their lips met and desire swept through her. She pushed at his jacket, eager to get to bare skin.

He lifted his head, breaking the kiss but keeping his lips close to hers. "We can't now, Breezy and Nightmare are waiting for us."

She nodded reluctantly. Of course he was right, but it did little to diminish her ardor. There seemed to be one distraction or problem after another since she arrived. Stepping away, she fought the urge to pout. "Let's go. Can't keep them waiting too long without Nightmare fretting." She teased, making her way across her large suite to the French double doors.

Storm waited for them in the hall. Farther down, Windwalker and Chameleon stood guard. She was surprised to find so many Enforcers for a family lunch. "Do we really need the extra Enforcers?"

"Nightmare's being cautious."

She leaned close, whispering so only Dreamer could hear. "Cautious of what? Me or the secret family relation?"

"Do I sense a note of jealousy, my Queen?" He smirked before sobering. "We didn't want to mention this to you now, but there's been some

196

activity in the town. A death threat delivered to the gatehouse, as well as some talk about an attack when you address the members of Storm Hollow. Nightmare planned to discuss this with you after lunch."

"Why?"

"We knew there would be some uproar from those who are still devoted to Queen Shower, as well as from enemies Nightmare and I have created over the years. We didn't expect the worst of the uproar to happen until after you've addressed your people, but someone saw Darkness here. Rumors are spreading like mad that he's here to kill anyone not loyal to you."

She stopped in her track, and turned toward him, her mouth agape. "That isn't the reason."

"We know that, but he's been an assassin for centuries. The Stormkins only see him as one thing. He instills fear in people. There's going to be some hostility and people will be terrified but once they realize why he's here it will bring you added protection, unless—"

"Unless his true desire *is* to kill me." She knew he didn't want to say it, didn't want to upset her, but it was what he was thinking.

"I apologize, my Queen, but yes I still have my doubts he can change." He laid his hand on hers.

"I know. People only change if they really want to. Only time will tell if he can, or will. In the meantime we'll be watching him. He's been given the only warning he'll receive from me. There's no going back if he steps out of line." She shook her head, trying to chase her worries away. Lately, all she could do was wonder what would go wrong next. "I have to address the community, they need to know why he's really here."

"Not until he's pledged his commitment. Let's go have lunch, in two short hours he'll be back and we can figure out the best way to handle the situation." He walked forward and she followed, her thoughts weighing her down.

Windwalker and Chameleon bowed their heads as she passed; Storm took his place beside Chameleon without question. Inside the living area, at the beginning of the hall that led toward their quarters, Breezy sat next to Nightmare, her long brown hair tied back from her face, the rest cascading down her neck in spiral curls. Her deep blue strapless dress, edged with white lace, made her look delicate and too innocent compared to her brothers. The sitting room was too girly for Kayla's taste. The sofa and chairs were white with big red and pink flowers printed all over them. Even the white shag throw rug in front of the sofa had pink trim around it. All she could think was, *the seventies called and want their room back.*

"Wow," she whispered more to herself than anyone in particular. "I'm sorry. Breezy, thank you for coming." Redecorating needed to go on the to-do list, stat.

"Thank you for having me, my Queen." She curtsied.

*Seriously, people still curtsy?* "Sit, visit with Dreamer. I apologize, but I need a moment with Nightmare." She nodded her head, calling Nightmare to her. "We'll only be a moment."

"Take as long as you need, my Queen." She hugged Dreamer, before pulling him down on the sofa with her.

It was good to see her men enjoying the company of their sister without having to watch over their shoulders. She kept that in mind as she stepped out, Nightmare on her heels. She didn't look back to make sure he followed until she was in the hall. Storm stepped away from the wall as if to follow. "No, Storm, stay there. We're just going down the hall."

Needing the privacy, she made her way back to her bedroom suite. With the door closed firmly behind them, she swung around to him, anger in her eyes. "Why didn't you tell me about the threats?"

"I didn't tell you because there's nothing you can do yet. We need to wait until Darkness has pledged himself to you. If we act on anything now, it will only make things worse."

"Another threat already, and you didn't think it was worth telling me? Damn it, they were at the gatehouse."

He advanced on her, and she stepped back. When she realized what she was doing, she stopped and held her ground. She wouldn't retreat; after all she was Queen here.

"As Queen, you'll have death threats," he told her. "It's part of ruling. It would be overwhelming to worry you with each threat. As for them being at the gate, they were in the house this morning. Why does it bother you so much they were at the gate?"

She thought about it for a moment, racking her brain. *Why does it bother me?* She couldn't come up with a reason. "I should have known they were here," she snapped.

"I won't apologize for protecting you, but I'll do my best to keep you informed of situations that arise in the future." He gave a small bow using just his head as though there wasn't room enough for anything more.

She wasn't sure why, but his tone—made it seem as if she didn't understand the ways of the world—only angered her further. She wasn't a child and would be damned if she'd be treated like one. "If I'm to rule then I need to know what dangers I'm facing. Sheltering me won't help me protect myself, nor will it make me happy."

"As your Enforcer in Charge my first duty is to keep you safe, above making you happy." He let out a deep breath, watching her as if he was waiting for her to lash out at him. "My Queen, it's been centuries since I had to balance the two. I was a green Enforcer the last time I had to."

"We're all on a learning curve." She raised her arm, reaching out to him.

"I'm only angry because I didn't know. How can I help protect myself if I don't know the dangers that are lurking behind the walls of the compound?"

"It's *our* job to protect you."

"But if I know what's happening I can assist in my protection instead of unknowingly fighting against you." She met his gaze, trying her best to convey the reason for her irritation. "I don't want any of us hurt."

"I'll keep you apprised in the future." He wrapped his arm around her back, their bodies fitting together like two pieces of a puzzle finally joined.

"Before we meet with Darkness to take his oath, I want Dreamer promoted to Lieutenant Enforcer. I think he needs to hear it come from you. He needs to know you think he's ready to lead."

"Okay, after lunch."

Wanting to gauge his reaction to her next suggestion, she studied him carefully. "Speaking of lunch, I think Breezy should move in here. Either to one of the empty rooms, or an Enforcer's cabin to give her more privacy."

His face remained stoic, but one eyebrow rose slightly in question. "What in the hell for?"

"I think she'll be safer here."

"Safer?" His voice rose slightly before he regained control. "All these years we have kept her safe, now you want to put her in the center of danger. I beg you my Queen, don't do this."

"If you'd hear me out, you'd understand the reason." She waited a brief moment, expecting Nightmare to interrupt her again. "Breezy is an amazing pastry chef and owns Stormy Treats. It would be logical that I'd want the best chefs close, especially since I'm sure it was clear last night I have a sweet tooth. She could be here, protected by the Enforcers, yet no one would think it was for anything other than my own indulgence in desserts."

She observed the lines on his forehead creasing, as if he were deep in thought. She continued, hoping she was swaying him. "I know you want her safe and right now things are unsteady in Storm Hollow. She's alone now that your father and his wife are serving under another Queen. If you want her to stay down there alone, with no one to watch over her, that's your choice, but I'm giving you a way to protect her without anyone knowing the real reason."

"It's truly an honor to serve you." He relented, his eyes twinkled with joy as he gave her the biggest smile she had seen from him yet. "Most wouldn't even consider Breezy's predicament. If she's in agreement, then I think it would be a good solution. I don't want to force it upon her."

"Very well. We should get back. We can discuss it with her, then I want you, Dreamer, and Breezy to have lunch. Storm will escort me back here." She slipped her arm from around him, stepping away.

He wrapped his hand around her wrist before she could escape him. "Darkness might have left for now but he'll be back soon, and until I trust him I want Dreamer or myself with you at all times."

"You've warded the place and I'm only going to be at the end of the hall. Storm will be with me. You two need to spend time with your sister and I'm worn out from earlier." She tried to slip her wrist from his grasp, but it only made him tighten his grip. It didn't hurt, but his fingers dug into her flesh.

"I want Windwalker and Chameleon with you as well, and I want them in this room. Storm can guard the door."

"Okay. Now let go of my wrist." He did as she asked and a red hand print marked her skin. She pulled down the sleeve of her sweater to cover it, before making her way to the door. She didn't wait for Nightmare as she marched back to the living room; he'd follow when he was good and ready.

A deep joyous laugh spilled out of the sitting room as she turned the corner to enter. Dreamer swung his gaze up to meet hers, laughter sparkling in his eyes. Since she met Dreamer she had never seen him as happy and carefree as he was now. Sadness filled her with the knowledge she might never have him in the blithe manner Breezy did. No matter their relationship he'd always be one of her Enforcers, his duty to protect her trumping all else.

"Ahh, Queen Kayla, come join us." Dreamer rose from his place beside his sister.

She stood there for a brief moment, listening to Nightmare give orders to the Enforcers in the hall, before moving across the room. Even walking across the short distance seemed to be more than she had energy for; it was like walking in sand, each step harder than the last.

"My Queen, are you all right?" Breezy reached for her hand when Kayla finally made it to the nearby chair, concern lacing her voice.

"I apologize, I'm just tired."

"I can come back..."

Kayla raised her hand. "No, honestly, it's fine. I want to speak with you about something important." She paused as Nightmare entered and closed the door. "I know your relation to them and I understand why you wish it to remain a secret."

Breezy's gaze went from Nightmare to Dreamer before falling back on Kayla. "It's not me who wishes to have my relation to them remain undisclosed, it was their idea. I'm proud to be their sister, even if it's only by partial relation. They are heroes to our kind, to Storm Hollow."

"I'll rephrase then. It would put you in jeopardy and that's the last thing any of us wish." She leaned forward, resting her elbows on her knees. "I would like you to stay on the grounds. You can take one of the suites here in the main house, or if you'd like more privacy you're welcome to make a home in one of the Enforcers' cabins."

"What in the world for? I have my own place now that Mom and Dad are gone."

"The coming months are going to be dangerous." Nightmare stepped closer, coming to stand next to her instead of slightly behind her. "It will be a treacherous time in Storm Hollow even without your connection being known. Queen Kayla has suggested this to keep you safe."

"But what about my business?"

Kayla forced a warm smile, trying hard to be welcoming despite her fatigue. "We're not asking you to close Stormy Treats. You can still have your life like you want, just living here. You'll be close to Nightmare and Dreamer, and you'll have the security of the grounds. No one would think twice as to why I want the best pastry chef close." She smirked, and this time it was genuine. "I'm sure it was clear last night that I *love* your desserts."

"I'd be happy to make you anything, at any time, no matter where I'm living. Please forgive me for speaking freely, but there's no reason for me to live here. I'm safe and I can take care of myself."

Nightmare stepped forward; Kayla could see the anger in his corded back muscles.

"Breezy, don't speak to our Queen like that," he scolded. "Remember the respect your parents taught you. We lost one sibling already. We can't afford to lose another, you need to be protected."

"Don't make this about Illusion's death," Breezy retorted. "I'm not out there risking my life like you do every day, I'm safe…as safe as anyone else in Storm Hollow."

Dreamer laid a hand gently on her leg. "We're just trying to protect you. I think it's a good idea, it's better than you living on the edge of town alone. I want you safe."

Kayla decided it was time to end the discussion before an argument broke out. "Breezy, I won't make it an order, it needs to be your decision. Think about it, meanwhile enjoy your lunch, and we'll speak again soon." She stood quickly, her head swimming. She would have fallen back in the chair if Nightmare hadn't been standing next to her; he caught her, his reflexes quick.

"What is it? Are you okay?" He slipped his arm around her waist to keep her on her feet.

"I'm fine…" The world starting spinning, making her ill. "I just need to lie down."

"Very well." He scooped her into his arms. "Go ahead and start lunch, I'm going to see to our Queen."

# Chapter Thirty-One

Kayla laid in her bed, staring at the ceiling, her stomach roiling. Something was wrong, but she couldn't think. Her brain worked overtime, her mouth was dry as if it'd been filled with cotton.

"My Queen." Nightmare sat on the corner of the bed, holding her hand.

"Something's…wrong." Her words came out in a slur, she wasn't even sure Nightmare could understand her.

"Just rest, Storm has gone to fetch the healer." With a gentle touch, he brushed her hair away from her face before drawing a slow line along her jaw.

Sharp pain exploded in her gut, as if a fire burned at full speed through her body. "What's wrong with me?" She gasped as if fighting for air.

"You've been poisoned. Damn it, I should have caught it before."

Anger flared to life in his eyes, matching the inferno burning within her. She wanted to do something, to say something that would quench it before it got out of hand but another wave of pain burst through her. He held her as her body convulsed in agony, tearing screams from her throat.

"Chameleon, get Dreamer! He can lessen her pain." Nightmare didn't turn around to look at Chameleon who stood by the door; he kept his attention on her.

"No." She cried out, causing Chameleon to look back at her with his hand on the knob. "Nightmare, he doesn't need to know. Let him enjoy his lunch." Her teeth were clenched in pain, making her words come out jumbled, but from his nod she gathered he understood.

"You heard the Queen, stand down." He slid his arm around her, pulling her close to his body. "Just bear with me a bit longer, the healer will be here soon."

She let out a loud cry, pain coursing through her, as the bedroom doors sprang open.

Storm entered with the woman, then took his position by the door as she rushed to the bed. "My Queen, I'm Starr, a healer. If I may?" She reached her hand out toward Kayla slowly, as if afraid she'd deny her touch.

Nightmare eased her back down, so Starr could examine her, but kept his hand wrapped around hers to comfort her. "She's been poisoned."

"I can see that. If you and the others will leave…"

"I'm the Queen's Enforcer in Charge, she goes nowhere without guards. You'll have to do what you must with us in the room." Nightmare sat, staring down at Kayla, never looking at the healer as if she didn't matter to him.

"The more auras I have to keep out of my circle of healing the longer it will take to heal her. If you could have the others step into the hall, I'll be able to heal her quickly. They can leave the door open, the space will allow me to focus better."

He thought about it for a moment and then nodded. "Chameleon, Storm, join Windwalker in the hall. Leave the door open."

"What's wrong with me?" Kayla croaked, her voice almost unrecognizable to her.

"As your Enforcer in Charge said, you've been poisoned. It was subtle at first making you weak most likely, until it could work its way through your body." She slipped onto the bed, crawling across it to sit cross-legged next to

Kayla. "Are you aware who attempted to kill our Queen?" She whispered to Nightmare as if she was afraid someone would overhear.

"I believe the poison was delivered by wind, so yes."

"It might not be my place to ask, but why then is *he* guarding her?" She shot a quick look to the doorway and Kayla could see the healer thought it was Windwalker who poisoned her.

"He isn't. The one who's done it, is dead. Now heal her, or leave."

Starr raised her arms, bringing her hands together, then gently rubbing them together before laying them on Kayla's stomach. Her eyes were closed as she focused on the task at hand. A warm glow began to grow between Kayla's stomach and the healer's hands. With each breath, the pain lessened until she breathed easy once again.

Collapsing back on the bed, her breath still coming in gasps as she tried to steady herself, she stared up at the two of them. "Thank you." She lost the battle to keep her eyes open, but still she clung to Nightmare's hand.

"My Queen, your Enforcer in Charge might not want to hear it but you need to know that you were poisoned by the wind…by someone's magical wind." Starr's voice was timid.

"I know." Still exhausted, her voice was low.

"You know and you let him guard you?"

She opened her eyes, thankful the world no longer spun, and took in the woman. Starr's long ebony hair flowed around her, silver strands woven throughout the darkness like stars in the sky. Her blue tank top and matching peasant skirt added a touch of color before blending nicely with her hair. The only contrast was her pale glowing skin.

"Starr, if you wish to retain your place in Storm Hollow I suggest you mind your own business. This does not concern you."

Nightmare swung around to look at Starr. Kayla was positive she'd find anger flaring to life in his eyes, yet he somehow managed to keep it out of his voice.

"I don't wish to leave my home, but I can't stand idly by while you let the man who tried to kill her continue to guard her. Next time I might be too late." She scooted to the edge of the bed, preparing to stand, but keeping an eye on him as if she didn't want to turn her back on him.

"You're either very brave or very stupid, I haven't figured out which yet," he grumbled. "I'm leaning toward stupid because you don't question your Queen or her Enforcer in Charge. You just do as you're told."

"Starr, Windwalker isn't the one who did this," Kayla insisted.

"The poison was delivered by wind—magical wind. There are very few in Storm Hollow who have that ability." Standing, Starr ran a hand over her skirt making sure it fell straight.

Kayla was beginning to tire of this repetitive conversation. She shouldn't have to explain things to this woman. "Thank you for removing the poison." She closed her eyes, leaning her head on the pillow. "Now Storm will escort you home."

# Chapter Thirty-Two

Kayla woke to find Nightmare sitting beside her bed, typing quietly on his laptop. Moonlight slivered through the room, painting his bare chest with its light.

"What time is it?" Tossing the blanket aside, she scooted up.

He closed his laptop, setting it aside on the nightstand. "It's just before eight o'clock."

"You shouldn't have let me sleep; there's much to deal with." She swung her legs over the side of the bed.

"Calm down, everything's fine. Dreamer has taken Darkness's sworn commitment to you as his Queen. Gideon heard of the attack and has just returned, Dreamer is taking his commitment as well and they'll both be settled into the barracks shortly. Meanwhile, I wrote up a statement we can have Ava deliver to the members of Storm Hollow."

"Ava? Who's she? Shouldn't I do it?"

"Ava has been Storm Hollow's director of events for many years. She's more than capable of handling this task. She has already begun to gather a list of Stormkins who will need to find another territory. If you feel well enough to attend the announcement ceremony, that can be arranged."

His long legs were stretched out in front of the chair, leaving her very little room to put her feet, so she remained sitting on the bed. "I feel fine. I should make the announcement. It might eliminate some concerns."

"Very well." He rose in one fluid motion, grasping her hands and pulling her to stand with him. "I apologize, my Queen, that I didn't catch the poison before."

"Starr said it was subtle, you couldn't have known." She cupped his cheek. "You told me before you could heal, why didn't you?"

"My ability is sexual. When intimate I can heal myself as well as my partner. You were not up for sexual activity, or I would have." He tugged her into an embrace.

"You'd always be my first choice as a healer." She kissed him, letting their tongues dance the dance of lovers before drawing away.

"Speaking of healers…Starr needs to learn her place or find another territory."

"Don't you think you're being a little hard on the girl? She's very young."

"No. If she's going to be your healer she needs to understand her place *now*. It will be harder to enforce it later. One day she'll say something that could get her killed." He looked down at her, their gazes meeting, and she could see the honesty clear in his eyes. "If she'd have said that in front of others, the situation could have gotten out of hand. We can't have your decisions questioned. Your community needs to realize when I speak, I'm speaking for you."

"Then deal with it." Stepping away she ran her hand through her hair before turning back to him. "I didn't mean to ruin your lunch with Breezy."

"There's a time for socializing and there's a time to be at my Queen's side." He slid his body closer to her, and there was a desire in his eyes she didn't see before. "I wouldn't have wanted to be anywhere else. Dreamer convinced Breezy to take one of the cabins; she'll move in tomorrow. So I'll see her again."

"Good, take tomorrow and see her. You need to reconnect with your sister."

"Connect," he mumbled.

"I thought…"

"Dreamer was always closest to her. Illusion and I were always busy when she was growing up, we rarely saw her."

She reached for him, slipping her hand into his. "Now's your chance. You deserve a life outside of your Enforcer duties."

"I have a life outside of it…I have you." His lips landed on her before she could tell him he needed more. He sought entry with his tongue and delved deeply into her mouth, as though trying to draw her in.

He broke the kiss, leaving her breathless. "I'll send for Ava, if you want to gather yourself."

Kayla had just finished reapplying her lipstick when a knock sounded at the door. She gave Nightmare a brief nod in the mirror and he went to open the door. A woman entered, her short curly blonde hair delicately framing her face. Her gray business suit and crème blouse made her look as if she should be a lawyer defending a high-class client.

"My Queen, it's a pleasure to finally meet you." She raised her arm, offering her hand to Kayla, as she circled the bed. "Though you don't know me yet, I hope you'll retain me as the director of your events."

*She's human.* Kayla wasn't sure how she could tell, but she was absolutely sure. Her ease about everything that was going on let her know Ava must have been in Shadow Providence for a long time. She was the first human Kayla found here. Suppressing her shock, she accepted the woman's hand. "Nightmare speaks highly of you."

Ava tossed him a quick smile, one that was more than just a thank you.

*Do they have a past together?* Kayla pushed the thought away for the moment, turning back to the issue at hand. "The statement that Nightmare gave you earlier, I'm going to deliver it."

"I delivered public statements from Queen Shower for years. I'm capable of dealing with it." Her voice never changed, but her eyes had a sadness that wasn't there before.

"I have no doubts you can, but as I have just taken control of this territory, I feel I should address my people. They need to recognize me as the ruler here. I would like you by my side."

"As my Queen wishes." She curtsied, looking at her watch. "If that's all, I need to see to a few things. Could you meet me in the entryway in ten minutes? We address the people just down the road at an outdoor stadium, because it's safer than having everyone here."

Nightmare nodded. "We'll see you there shortly." He escorted her to the door, reaching it just as Dreamer opened it.

Dreamer's eyes lit with joy when his gaze landed on Kayla. "My Queen, you're all right." He wrapped his arms around her, pulling her tight. There was a safeness in his embrace that she enjoyed, his toned body pressed firmly against her, and she relaxed. He ran his hands down her back as if he was trying to convince himself she was there, that nothing had happened to her.

"Dreamer…" Her words were silenced as he squeezed her tightly again.

Nightmare stood with his back against the closed bedroom door, watching them. "Dreamer, she's fine, but if you continue squeezing the life out of her I'll have to get the healer back. Trust me when I say…I *don't* want to deal with Starr again today."

Dreamer loosened his hold, adjusting so she was more on the side of his body, but his arm was still around her waist as he held her snuggly. "What was Ava doing here? I thought she was giving the announcement."

"Our Queen sees fit to deliver the message herself. We'll be leaving in ten minutes."

"Ava's human…" She waited for one of them to fill in the blanks.

"She's been here too long to leave now. Humans age slower here. If she left now, all the years would catch up to her and she'd die." There was no compassion in Nightmare's voice, just a simple statement, as if he didn't care she could never return to her homeland.

"She's appears to be in her late thirties."

"Ava came here long before your father left. She married one of the ground Enforcers, before he was killed on a mission. She chose to remain here and is a very valuable member of our community. She has asked to stay on and continue in her role as director of events. It will be your decision but I think it would be wise to allow her. She has gained the respect of the members of Storm Hollow and is talented at her job."

"I have no issue with her remaining in her position, I was just stunned she's human." She let her hand fall away from Dreamer's chest but didn't step out of his embrace. "Nightmare, when I address Storm Hollow, I want you on my right, Ava on my left. Dreamer, I want you and Darkness directly behind me. The other Enforcers can stand behind them, or wherever you want them, Nightmare. But I want us to look like a strong core and Darkness, even though we don't completely trust him yet, needs to be with us since we'll be discussing his presence in Storm Hollow."

"You've been busy thinking about it." Nightmare smiled at her.

"I have. We've received death threats already, we need to appear as united and resilient as possible. The slightest flaw could equal destruction, you've told me that repeatedly. Those against us will seek our weakest point and take advantage of it."

"You're quickly stepping into your position as Queen and you're doing a wonderful job."

"Shall we go then?" She stepped away from Dreamer and looked back at the mirror to make sure she was presentable.

"In a moment." He looked from her to Dreamer. "Dreamer, I want you to take the position of Lieutenant Enforcer."

Dreamer gasped and swung around to stare at her. "Whose idea was this?"

"Nightmare's, but I completely agree. You'd be perfect for this. Without being harsh, do you know why I chose Nightmare as my Enforcer in Charge?"

He raised his eyebrow in question. "He's perfect for the job, I could list a hundred reasons why. You couldn't have made a better choice."

She sat on the plush white vanity. "You *both* would have been a good choice. Both of you carry an air of confidence like a second skin, but you look to Nightmare for reassurance. There's nothing wrong with that, that's the only thing that separated you two when it came to the position. You trust him implicitly and follow his orders already."

"You'd be my second," Nightmare said. "If anything happens to me, you would have to step up and protect Kayla. There's no one else I'd trust to keep her safe." When Dreamer continued to looked as though they just dumped a bucket of ice water over him. "You wouldn't want someone else to take the position. You'll keep Kayla safe like no other. We both know that."

Dreamer swallowed, his eyes returning to normal, and nodded. "You're right, there's no one else I trust to keep her safe. I'll do it."

"Then let's go. Ava will be waiting." She uncrossed her legs, gently rising to stand on the stiletto heels she'd slipped on.

"I won't let you down, my Queen," Dreamer promised.

"I know." She stepped toward him, and placed a gentle kiss on his lips.

# Chapter Thirty-Three

Butterflies danced in Kayla's stomach as she stepped up to the podium. It seemed as if the whole town had gathered and stared up at her, making her nervous. She had never been comfortable with talking in front of large crowds, but she wanted to do this. It only made things worse knowing there were people in the crowd who wished her harm.

Having her men in attendance gave her the courage to continue. She needed to establish herself in the eyes of the people.

Ava leaned into the microphone and all mumbles of conversations died. "Ladies and Gentlemen, thank you for coming this evening. Our Queen has a few announcements she'd like to deliver and then you're more than welcome to stay after and join us for coffee. Breezy, from Stormy Treats, has made some delicious finger desserts for everyone." Stepping back, the human bowed her head to Kayla—demonstrating her loyalty.

Swallowing the lump in her throat, Kayla reached for the microphone. "Thank you for coming. Many of you saw Darkness arrive earlier today and there have been rumors I have brought him here to hunt down my enemies. This is not the case. Darkness has come to Storm Hollow seeking a place in service. Earlier this afternoon he took the oath as one of my elite Enforcers. He will be no threat to—"

"No threat, that's bullshit!" a man from the crowd shouted. "People, don't succumb to the brainwashing, he's here to kill us. Anyone who doesn't follow her orders to the letter will end up at *his* mercy."

Everything began to slip downhill from there, and a lump rose in her throat.

Chameleon and Thunder closed in on the man who started the disturbance, as others began shouting out, some in support and others against her.

"We should leave, let Ava handle the rest." Nightmare slid his arm behind her, his hand gently resting on the small of her back.

"Go, my Queen," Ava urged. "I'll get things under control and finish the announcement. Your safety is most important." Ava raced toward the microphone—whether to take control or provide another target, Kayla had no idea.

She looked up at Nightmare when things suddenly went from bad to worse.

"Down!" Darkness pushed them to the ground before falling on top of them. Bullets sliced the air, the sounds slamming against Kayla's eardrums.

Under Darkness's arm she could see Storm and Windwalker dealing with those rushing the podium, while Dreamer crouched near, his gun drawn.

"We've got to get the Queen out of here. Nightmare, get her to safety, I'll watch your back." Dreamer rose, using himself as a shield, seconds before Nightmare and Darkness pulled her to her feet.

Dreamer spoke breathlessly just as he pushed them toward the steps: "*Bomb.*"

She wasn't able to see much because she was almost completely shielded by their bodies, when all of a sudden the platform shook. The bang was deafening; there was blood everywhere, covering her, and she didn't know where it'd come from.

The front of her pale pink sweater had turned deep burgundy, wet and pungent, while chunks of gore surrounded them where they stood.

She took a quick look back wondering how Ava faired because she couldn't find her in the chaos. The only thing her mind would register was the pile of ashes just a few feet from where they'd been only moments before.

Everything else was a blur; she couldn't recognize any of the faces that surrounded her except Nightmare and Dreamer. She knew the other men, but in that moment they could have been strangers. She clung to Nightmare, wishing she could do the same with Dreamer but he was steps behind, watching their backs.

*Dreamer*, she cried out in her mind, wishing he was with her too. He turned and looked at her as if he'd heard her. Their gazes met through the crowds of people running—trying to escape—as she watched his eyes widen in question, when he turned toward her. *Did he hear me? How is that even possible?*

"Go, I'm right behind you," Dreamer directed, and turned back to help the Enforcers clear the podium. They were beginning to gain control over the area, the shooter was subdued, and Ava tried to calm the remaining Stormkins.

The noise grew distant while Nightmare practically carried her to the car. Screams no longer filled the air, drowning her with their sorrow. When she looked behind them she could no longer see Dreamer and concern flowed through her like an unwanted chill.

"Come, my Queen. Dreamer and the others will be fine. It's you they're—" The rest of his words died on his lips as the ground once again shook beneath her feet. The loud explosion sent them stumbling backward, trying to get away from the car—her SUV—as it exploded before her.

"We must go back." In less than an hour, she had three attempts on her life. One or more of her people were intent on killing her. They needed to find out who—*now*. "We have to go back."

"What the hell for? People are trying to *kill* you." Nightmare turned to her, his expression full of outrage.

"I have to show I rule here. No one will be able to force me into hiding, or scare me from ruling Storm Hollow. They need to understand the price for such behavior. I won't stand by idly and let someone repeatedly threaten my life. Today I'll prove it to them." She wouldn't run, she was tired of living in fear.

"My Queen, we need to get you to safety."

"No, Nightmare. There'll never be anywhere safe as long as the people who attacked tonight remain in Storm Hollow." She looked over her shoulder at Nightmare who kept pace with her. "Are you coming with me? As my Enforcer in Charge you should be with me."

"I'd never let you go alone, but are you sure you want to do this now?"

"There's no better time than now. I'll make an example of them."

Her ears ringing, she headed back the way they'd come, and strode out onto the stage.

"The situation is now under control. If everyone will please take their seats I can finish the announcement the Queen intended to give." Ava stood at the podium, her back to Kayla. Ava's gray business suit and crème blouse were splattered with blood.

Kayla glided up next to her, moving the microphone slightly so her voice would be heard over the bustle of the crowd. "Ava's correct. If everyone would please return to their seats I'd like to deal with a few issues."

She waited for everyone to settle, and the crowd hushed.

"Tonight you witnessed two attempts on my life, what you didn't witness was the third. You already know death is the punishment for an attempt on a Queen's life. The guilty parties will face the consequences soon. Effective immediately, anyone who threatens, attacks, or kills a half-breed, will also meet the same punishment. Storm Hollow might be the only place where half-breeds and unwanted Stormkins are welcome but this law will be in effect for all Stormkins residing or visiting here. I will not tolerate prejudice of any sort in my territory. If you cannot live among those who are different than you, it's time for you to find another territory to call your home."

The crowd rumbled its displeasure, but there was no repeat of the earlier outrage. Either they valued their lives or they were biding their time.

She turned her body slightly, looking across the podium where her Enforcers held two men, kneeling. Windwalker stood behind the first man, holding a fistful of his hair, yet the man still struggled against him. His hands were chained in front of him, the links running down to the floor and disappearing between his legs where she assumed he was restrained by leg irons.

"What is your name?" she demanded.

"Kill me and get it over with. But the T.S.K. won't rest until you and the rest of your half-breed bitches are dead!"

"T.S.K.?"

"True Stormkins. They'll see your head on a platter long before you can complete the prophecies."

She looked back at Windwalker, his drawn sword pointed toward the ground. She held out her hand, thankful for the weapons' training her father made her take years ago. In that instant it hit her...*Dad knew all along I'd be here one day, and that training would come in handy. Why else would he make me take it?*

*Humans prefer guns to swords.*

"Windwalker, give me your sword." She loved that he didn't hesitate, didn't ask her if she knew how to use it. He just held it out to her, hilt first. "I ask you again, what is your name?"

The man knelt there, his gaze locked on hers, refusing to answer. She wanted to know his name before she killed him, but in the end it didn't really matter. She'd kill him regardless.

"His name is Tornado. Him and his son, T.J., came to Storm Hollow a few months ago." A young, silver-haired man rose from the middle of the crowd, his voice shaky as if afraid he'd be punished for speaking out.

"You are?"

"Winter Thaw, my Queen." He gave a small bow, taking care not to bump into the person in front of him.

"How do you know them?"

"I have an isolated cabin out in the woods. They reside in one just down the path. They kept to themselves but you could tell they were training for something, and always at the oddest hours as if they were worried someone would observe them."

She let his words sink in, with the haunting feeling they had been plotting to go to war against half-breeds, before turning her attention back to the person she now knew as Tornado.

"Do you have any last words?" She raised the sword, preparing for the killing blow. Windwalker stepped back and out of the way of her striking zone.

"I'll see you in hell, bitch." Anger coursed through his words but he didn't struggle against his bonds. He faced death with courage.

Tornado's gaze never left hers as she swung the sword with all the strength she possessed. She knew the Enforcers kept their swords sharp and ready for any threat that presented itself, but she was still slightly surprised when the blade cut cleanly through his neck.

His head plopped to the ground with a wet thump, blood squirting from his neck, covering her and everyone near. His body turned to dust swiftly.

She used the back of her hand to wipe the blood from her cheek, and moved to the younger man. Tears streaked his face, and she wasn't sure if it was for the loss of his father or his pending demise. "T.J., you were the one who threw the bomb at me. Did you also add the one to my SUV with the intent to kill me if you didn't succeed here?"

"Yes." He rose to his feet and stumbled toward her.

Dropping the sword, she stretched out her hand and called the lightning. It tingled its way through her body, working itself down her hands before springing free from her fingertips and hitting him dead center in his chest. His body shuddered before crumbling and turning to dust.

For a moment she stood there, looking down at the two piles of dust, letting the realization that she'd just added two more to her kill list sink in, before turning back to the watching Stormkins.

"I won't tolerate any treason from my own people. If you don't approve of how I run Storm Hollow, this is your chance to leave. I won't be lenient on anyone who attacks me, my Enforcers, or the members of my community—no matter their heritage or background. If I see you as a threat you'll be dealt with accordingly. Anyone who doesn't want to remain in Storm Hollow has twenty-four hours to leave. Shadow Mother has arranged for you to travel there until you find another home."

She glanced around the stadium. "Those who wish to stay, know this…there will be major restructuring of the community to make a safe place for everyone, half-breeds and unwanted Stormkins included. Tonight's not the time to go over these changes, but announcements will be forthcoming, either by Ava or myself."

With that, she stepped away from the microphone, her men forming a protective circle as she strode from the area.

"Storm fetched a new SUV," Dreamer whispered to her as they made their way out, before giving her hand a quick squeeze. "Let's get you home."

# Chapter Thirty-Four

Kayla waited in the hallway with Dreamer and Darkness as Nightmare searched her suite. It was unlikely anything had been placed in the suite but no one was taking any chances. When Nightmare came out of the bathroom he gave the all clear to Dreamer and Darkness, allowing them to bring her in. Dreamer entered beside her, neither of them touching, as if they didn't want to risk adding more blood to their already blood-soaked clothes. Her ruined sweater clung to her body as she tried to pull it over her head.

Her white bra was no better, now stained red, but at least it didn't cling to her skin the way the sweater did. Soon it wouldn't matter. Now that she was home, she could shower, put on fresh clothes, and throw these away.

"I need a shower…" Her words were cut off by a chirping coming from the mirror as the glass began to swirl. "Who could that be?"

"My guess would be Shadow Mother. She couldn't have heard about what happened already." Nightmare stepped over to the mirror as the sound grew louder. "You'll have to answer."

A deep sigh escaped her lips, and her shoulders sank; the hot shower would have to wait. She nodded, moving into direct view of the mirror. Dreamer followed, coming to stand a step behind her, while Darkness stayed close to the door, out of view. "Go ahead, Nightmare."

He touched the mirror, bringing forth the vision of Shadow Mother, her hair piled nicely on top of her head, the green dress appearing formal, as loud music played in the distance. Nightmare stepped up to Kayla, never turning his back on Shadow Mother.

"Shadow Mother, what an unexpected—"

"Don't placate me, child. Tonight we were having a celebration. It should have been a happy occasion as I've killed one of my greatest adversaries. It was until things turned disturbing when one of my guests informed me that Darkness was in your territory—as *yours*. Is this true?" Anger glowed in Shadow Mother's eyes.

"Yes, Darkness has sought a place within my command, and he's taken a place as an Enforcer. Is there some issue I'm unaware of?" She tried to keep her tone even.

"The *problem* is that Darkness is one of the most sought after assassins the Stormkins have. He cannot just walk away from his duties and expect there to be no consequences."

"My Queen, if I may." Darkness called to her out of the view of the mirror.

"Yes, come here, Darkness." Kayla held her hand out to him. They needed to show Shadow Mother they were united and she fully supported his decision to join her Enforcers.

The assassin took her hand obligingly. His face angled at her, clearly asking if she understood what that small gesture would tell Shadow Mother. She gave his hand a squeeze, to let her eyes convey her approval. He must have understood because he turned to the mirror and spoke freely.

"I have left no loose ends, Shadow Mother, before coming to Queen Kayla. I made sure all my commitments were complete. There are others who can be called on to handle anything you and the other Queens need dealt with."

"You'll report to Hurricane's Gentle Care by sunup—"

Kayla was quick to interrupt. "Shadow Mother, he's taken a position with me. He has done *nothing* to deserve this." There had been three attempts on her life that night and she stood covered in blood from head to toe, so she had no patience for Shadow Mother's games. She wouldn't lose one of the men who'd helped save her only a short time before.

"Kayla, you speak out of turn. You are a Queen and I can't send you to Hurricane's Gentle Care, but I can make things difficult for you."

Nightmare took a step forward, taking the brunt of Shadow Mother's attention. "The laws of the Stormkin strictly state that once a Queen has claimed an Enforcer no one else can order him away, unless they have broken a law. Darkness has done nothing against our laws."

"Have you claimed Darkness in the same way you have Nightmare and Dreamer?" Shadow Mother's gaze returned to Kayla.

"That is not required with all Enforcers." Nightmare spoke up trying to bring the attention back on himself.

"No, not on all. I looked the other way when you brought Windwalker to your land, but I won't do it with Darkness. Either you take Darkness to your bed to claim him, or he shall report to Hurricane's Gentle Care. That's your choice."

"Yes, Shadow Mother."

"I'll be out of touch tomorrow so if he doesn't appear at Hurricane's Gentle Care I'll assume you've claimed him. If I find out otherwise, I'll demand Darkness's life for disobedience. You might also forfeit the lives of your other men. Keep that in mind as you continue to add powerful warriors to your land." With those final words the mirror once again turned solid.

She had about all she could stand of the games Shadow Mother insisted on playing. Especially tired of Shadow Mother deciding who she slept with.

There had to be something she could do about it, because she was damn sure she wouldn't let Shadow Mother continue to threaten her with the men she loved.

They stood there in silence, waiting for the other shoe to drop, until Kayla spoke up. "What is Hurricane's Gentle Care?"

A look of horror crossed over each of the men's faces before Nightmare finally answered. "Hurricane is Shadow Mother's torturer. He carries out all the punishments. Other Queens also send their people to him if they don't wish to handle it themselves. His true joy is torture and blood."

It made her sick to think of such a place and from the looks she received from them when it was mentioned she knew they had all spent time there.

*Never again!* She vowed, unwilling to see her men tortured. Even with her distrust in Darkness, she didn't want to see him end up there. She'd do what was asked to save him. *Funny how I vowed I wouldn't be a whore for Shadow Mother, yet here I am adding a third man to my bed.*

"We all need a shower." Kayla ran her hand through her hair, wanting badly to cleanse herself of the gruesomeness she'd just experienced. "Nightmare, come with me. You two can get cleaned up and report back here in thirty minutes." She scurried off to the bathroom desperate to get the blood off her skin, not caring if Nightmare followed her or not. There was no doubt in her mind he wouldn't leave her unguarded, especially not after the attempts on her life tonight.

The tile was cool against her bare feet as she entered the large bathroom, but it was the mirror above the counter that caught her attention. She almost looked over her shoulder expecting another woman to be standing there, until she realized it was her reflection. Empty, hollow eyes stared back at her surrounded by blood stains

Nightmare stepped into view of the mirror, watching her. "Are you okay?"

She didn't know how to answer that. To say she was fine would imply she didn't care she'd just killed two men, a father and son—a family. With no answer to give, she peeled away the fouled clothes.

He stalked to her as though she were prey, but his eyes held desire. Desire and love.

She did the only thing she could, she focused on him. "You're injured."

"I'll be fine."

She knew he'd heal with time, but there was a quicker way and she wanted to find out just how his sexual healing ability worked. "Join me in the shower."

"I'll clean up once Dreamer is back. You need an armed Enforcer with you at all times."

"You won't let anything happen to me. I know you left Windwalker and Chameleon guarding the door while the others clean up. Join me." She ran her hand up his shirt; unlike hers, his was still wet with blood—his blood—as it dripped down from the wound on his shoulder. But a little extra blood didn't matter to her, only his injury mattered.

He stripped out of his clothes while she turned on the shower. When steam rose from the stall, she stepped in, letting the hot water cascade down her body. She closed her eyes, putting her head under the powerful showerhead, allowing the water to rinse away the blood that had begun to harden in her hair.

Steam billowed around her, escaping above the glass shower door when Nightmare opened it to step in. "Damn." He yelped as the hot water hit his skin.

"Too hot?"

"Are you trying to boil yourself alive and save your enemies the trouble of killing you?"

Unamused, she turned down the temperature. "Better?"

He used his body to answer her, stepping closer, joining her under the water's spray. His lips crushed against hers with such force she'd have stumbled if he didn't have his arm around her waist. He tasted like the air after a summer rain, spicy and full of promise. His hands ran down the length of her body, exploring every curve, as his tongue invaded her mouth and claimed it.

Breaking the kiss, she murmured, "I want you, now."

Facing death left her with no interest in foreplay and thankfully, he seemed to feel the same way. Lifting her, he pushed her against the tile and thrust inside her with one continuous motion. The world narrowed to the pump action of his shaft sliding in and out of her. She clung to him, the water making his skin hot and slippery.

Burying his face against her neck, his hips pistoned against her, every stroke amping up her pleasure until an orgasm stormed through her system. She held onto him as a second one crashed through her and then a third and still he pounded her relentlessly. The world shattered and came together and then blew apart a fourth time when his body went rigid and he spilled his release inside of her.

The wave of his orgasm seemed to merge with hers and she shuddered with the force of it. A faint plink brought her back to the present and she stared at the bullet swirling in the water near the drain. His shoulder wound was gone, the skin solid and toned as if it had never been broken.

"You're healed." Breathless amazement filled her. He'd told her his ability, but knowing and seeing were two different things.

"I told you I heal through sex. Look, your shoulder is healed as well."

He was right; the burn from the bomb had been erased, leaving only smooth unmarred skin.

"Wow. That ability is great."

He kissed her neck again before lowering her back to her feet. "It will come in handy to keep my Queen safe, of that I am sure."

# Chapter Thirty-Five

She sat on the sofa looking at the three men who were discussing her evening activities as if she wasn't there. She couldn't believe she was listening to them banter about her sex life, attempting to negotiate something that was normally kept private. Nightmare refused to allow Darkness alone with her, and Darkness refused to perform with an audience. They were at an impasse.

Without an agreement, Darkness would be reporting to Hurricane's Gentle Care; it didn't seem to bother anyone, making her wonder which Darkness would prefer. Did he see having sex with a half-breed Queen worse than surrendering himself to Hurricane's torture?

It was time to end the discussion. When she rose, the men fell silent. "Darkness, either Dreamer stays with us or you can report to Hurricane's Gentle Care tonight. Nightmare, you and whoever else you trust most will be guarding the door until Darkness leaves the room for the night. That's it. Take it or don't, but it's been a long day and I'm tired of this. I want to get this done and get some sleep."

"As my Queen wishes." Nightmare's tone was even, but amusement crept into his eyes. He gave her a small bow before making his exit.

She knew he'd stay just outside of the door unless he sensed the slightest hint of danger. He was her safety net. The cool silk of her emerald green nightshirt clung to her body as she sauntered toward the bed, grabbing

Dreamer's hand with the hopes that once he joined her, Darkness would follow. "Come, the night grows late."

She wanted to play now that her wild desire had been satiated by Nightmare's passion in the shower. Working the buttons of his shirt open, she reveled in exploring Dreamer's chest. Tracing her fingers over his scars, she pushed the shirt wider and kissed them. Dreamer shook with the first brush of her lips, so she indulged herself and traced the length of one scar with her tongue. Awareness slithered through her, an almost hedonistic pleasure.

Darkness watched them.

Kissing a path down his chest to his belly, she worked his pants open and stepped back.

"Strip." Confidence flowered in her belly. She knew how to demand what she wanted from her lovers, but she'd never been so bold as to take full command. He discarded his clothes and then reached for her again.

Despite his earlier reservations about Darkness, he didn't seem to give a damn as the assassin devoured their every move with his eyes. Her nightdress ripped and Dreamer tumbled her onto the bed. Her body, still relaxed and warm from Nightmare's lovemaking, went weak at the feel of Dreamer's hard shaft pressing against her belly.

He kissed her, a long, slow deliberate kiss that gave and demanded. He cupped her breasts and teased the nipples, gently swirling his thumbs against the hard buds and then pinching them. Pain mingled with pleasure and her back arched. She forgot who was supposed to be in control. His warm laughter washed over her and he abandoned her mouth, sucking one nipple against his teeth.

Sparks of pleasure fired inside of her. He slid his hand between her thighs, urging them apart and just when she thought he would take her, he teased her and wrenched an orgasm from her.

She cried out at the unexpected climax as the air sizzled around her and he drove her toward the brink again. Turning her head, her pleasure-soaked gaze found Darkness.

"Come." She'd almost forgotten what the night was all about. Something shredded his control because he stalked toward the bed, stripping his clothes as he went. The moonlight glistened off his pale skin and his shaft bounced against his belly, hard and swollen.

Liquid heat melted through her and she stretched out a hand to caress the length of it.

Aware that Dreamer stared at her, his fingers gliding back and forth against her wet folds, she turned and took Darkness's length in her mouth.

A hard inhale of breath came from each man. Drunk on the need to have them both, she swirled her tongue around the tip, sucking it hard. The assassin groaned, and reached down to cup the back of her head tentatively. He didn't try to urge her, allowing her to set the pace.

If he came in her mouth, it would not satisfy Shadow Mother. To give him the opportunity, the privilege Dreamer and Nightmare shared, she needed to trust him. She couldn't allow him between her legs, not with the chance of child—the chance he could be King to her Queen.

She wanted to trust him, but settled for pleasuring him. He was in her bed; it would have to be enough. Easing her mouth away, she looked to Dreamer who awaited her pleasure. His shaft was dark and thick, eagerly straining toward her.

"Take me," she ordered. He slid into her with one powerful thrust. Her core ached from Nightmare's earlier eagerness, but was so sensitive she nearly came again. The position was difficult and as if sensing her need, Dreamer slid free and turned her over.

He lined up behind her and she shuddered with the contact as he thrust into her from the back, his hips slapping against her ass. Darkness moved to face her and she caught his shaft and pulled it into her mouth again. Their rhythm quickly synced allowing them to find pleasure as one, rocking together in perfect harmony.

Waves of ecstasy engulfed them, and Darkness was the first to cry out as he filled her mouth with his cum. She writhed beneath Dreamer, swallowing Darkness's juices as another wild climax spiraled through her.

Dreamer cried out as he slammed home a final time and came in a jet of liquid gold that seemed to fill her being. They collapsed together. Dreamer spooned against her back, but her head rested against Darkness's belly. Tilting her head up, she met his wondering gaze and smiled.

They had finally had the time to build trust between them.

# Chapter Thirty-Six

Hours before sunrise, Darkness retired to his own room, leaving Kayla and Dreamer alone. She woke to what she had come to consider daylight—which in truth was more like dusk—shining through her windows.

"What is it?" Dreamer's voice was thick with sleep.

She ran her hand over his toned chest, feeling the way the muscles tightened under his skin. "I was just thinking. What time is it?"

"A little after seven, why?"

She frowned, wishing it was later. She had never been an early morning person. "I was wondering if Nightmare would be up yet."

"Tired of me already?" He teased. Though he said nothing, she knew he took pleasure in the fact that although Darkness shared their bed for much of the night, she never let him between her thighs.

"Never." She kissed his cheek. "I just had some things I wanted to go over, so it seemed sensible to have both of you here, instead of having to go over it twice."

He reached for his cell phone, hit a button and brought it to his ear. "Our Queen would like to see you." It was all he said before he ended the call and sat it back on the nightstand.

He was short and to the point and she liked that. No need to tip-toe around when it came to Dreamer. He'd always be straight forward with her, even if it was something she didn't really want to hear.

Expecting to have some time before Nightmare arrived, she hadn't wiggled from Dreamer's embrace when the bedroom suite doors open. Nightmare stood before her in a pair of worn blue jeans and nothing else. His chest still had lines from where the sheets were pressed against them, and his hair was tousled from sleep.

"My Queen, you requested my presence?"

"I apologize for the time. I was awake and thinking about Winter Thaw. What do you know about him?" She scooted up in the bed, resting her back against the plush headboard, keeping the sheet tight against her chest.

He sat on the edge of the bed closest to her. "He was an Enforcer but when Queen Lisa took over she feared his abilities and left him be. She let him keep his cabin in the woods with the understanding if he caused any problems he'd be exiled."

"What are his abilities?"

"He has the ability to thaw ice under someone's feet only to refreeze it with them on the other side. It won't kill a Stormkin, but it would be an eternity of never breathing air again. You'd just be stuck in the water like an ice cube, never finding a way out."

His words sent chills through her. She'd rather burn at the hands of a Sunkin than be trapped like that and never die.

Dreamer ran his hand over her thigh chasing away the goosebumps that formed. "He can bespell you with his eyes if he wishes, making you think you're in a winter wonderland meanwhile you're in a desert dying. If he bespells someone, it's to their death."

When Nightmare spoke again she couldn't help but notice they played off each other very well, filling in blanks the other left open. "Don't get us wrong, not all of his abilities are as bad as they sound. He can shoot icicles from his fingertips, even on the warmest day. He's a worthy Enforcer, and when he's committed to a Queen he'll serve her with his last breath. Those he's against, he'll fight them until they're are dead. After last night I think he could be a strong supporter of yours. Why do you ask about him?"

"The way he spoke up caught my attention. Send Darkness to fetch him, I want to speak with him."

"My Queen, I don't think sending Darkness would be the best choice, many still see him as a threat. Winter Thaw might react without thinking it through if Darkness appeared on his doorstep unannounced."

Nightmare had a good point; she didn't need someone to kill Darkness when she'd only just saved him. "Very well. Send someone else."

"I'll have Thunder go, but if you don't mind me asking, what are your plans when Winter Thaw arrives?"

"You have told me I need more Enforcers, I'm trying to do just that. We'll also need to find someone in charge of construction."

"Construction?" Dreamer rose to his elbow, looking up at her in question.

"I know there are houses within the community available for new members. But I also want to build a kind of condominium building for half-breeds only. This will give them a sense of security, as well as company of others like themselves. It will be guarded round the clock. The new members of Storm Hollow will need to feel this is a safe haven." She scooted to the edge of the bed, feeling the coolness of the wood floor under her feet as she stood. "When you send Thunder to find Winter Thaw, tell Ava I need a list of any areas capable of construction."

"Yes, my Queen. I'll just dress first."

"Very well, and when you're done, come back here and we can work out some other things." She needed to tell him what she'd realized last night; he had to know he wasn't the only one questioning Darkness's loyalty.

A cool wind blew through her hair. No matter how big her new mansion was, she was tired of being inside, staring at the same walls. She'd gone over new designs for the rooms with Ava earlier in the day and she promised she'd get a team to redecorate soon; they'd start with her bedroom suite before working their way down the hall, and into the rest of the house.

Dreamer opened the French doors to the patio and stepped out to join her and Nightmare. "My Queen, Winter Thaw has arrived."

"Bring him to me and join us," Nightmare told Dreamer, as he closed the notebook they had been using to write down some of the changes they were planning for Storm Hollow.

Winter Thaw stepped out onto the patio with Dreamer following behind him. His long silver hair was tied back at the nape of his neck, otherwise he looked the same as he had last night. The same black shirt was tight against his chest, pulling over the contours of his muscles. Were all Enforcers cut from the same demi-god mold?

She was beginning to understand why Queens took as many lovers as they wished. They were surrounded by beefcake.

"My Queen, you've requested to see me. What can I do for you?"

"Sit down." She nodded to the vacant chair across from her. "I called you here because last night you spoke out and helped."

"I meant no disrespect, I only did it to assist you." He sat, his gaze not quite meeting hers yet.

"Your reason is noble, and I've learned a lot about you this morning. Queen Lisa left you be because she feared you, but she's no longer here. Do you have a desire to serve as an Enforcer here in Storm Hollow? Or possibly find another territory to serve in?"

He looked to Nightmare for a moment before looking back at her. "Nightmare and I go back centuries, I was with him when he learned of the prophecies concerning you, but unlike him I never believed it. I never sought you out because I didn't believe there would ever be someone to redeem us from what we've come to be. We have fallen a great deal and if something isn't done we'll lose the battle against the Sunkins, leaving humanity without any defense."

"That doesn't answer my question, Winter Thaw."

"I apologize, my Queen. I'm still in shock that someone will save us. I've been living in the woods, not dealing with any of the problems of the Stormkins but depressed over the decline of what we once were. I'd be honored to serve you, to do whatever I can to help bring the Stormkins back to as strong as we once were, but I want to remain in my own cabin for now."

"Very well. Nightmare's my Enforcer in Charge, and Dreamer's the Lieutenant Enforcer. You'll report directly to them. Nightmare will take care of your commitment to me as well as give you your duties. Dreamer and I have something we're going to attend to. Welcome aboard, but know if you step out of line there will be severe consequences."

She didn't spare him another look as she rose and walked back inside.

"Where are we going?" Dreamer asked.

"Nowhere. Nightmare has history with him, he'll be able to get the information out of Winter Thaw."

"What?"

She turned her head away from the window and looked at Dreamer. "Winter Thaw hasn't been living in the woods, surrounded by so much snow and ice, for no reason. He's trying to keep people out...he's protecting someone." At his quizzical look, she shrugged. "I heard something someone said last night and that got me thinking about it, but it wasn't until he mentioned that he wanted to stay in the woods that I was certain. Nightmare picked up on it as well, he'll find out what he's hiding. If not we'll search his forest until we know." She tucked a strand of hair behind her ear. "Did Breezy get settled in?"

"Yes. She moved in with some of her stuff, mostly just personal things. She refuses to give up her home. But at least for now, she's safe."

She squeezed Dreamer's hand hoping to ease his worry about Breezy. "I understand her wanting to keep her home. Anything could happen and someday she might need it. Hopefully in the near future Storm Hollow will be safe enough to allow her to return if that's what she wishes."

# Chapter Thirty-Seven

Nightmare entered the house, leaving Winter Thaw sitting alone on the patio. "I haven't taken his commitment yet. You were right. He's hiding someone at his cabin, but he won't tell me who."

"We'll see about that." She pushed back open the door, and strolled back to the table where he sat, careful not to catch her heel in one of the cracks. "Winter Thaw, I believe you have great potential as an Enforcer for me, but if you can't be upfront with me then I can't trust you. I know you're hiding something at your cabin, and if you're not prepared to tell me then you can remain in one of the cells downstairs until I'm able to find out."

"My Queen, you don't understand what you're asking." A deep sadness coated his words, along with a touch of fear.

"I'm not making you choose. If it's something we can look past then we will. But I won't stand for an unknown security risk in my land. You'll be detained until we can get to the bottom of the situation, and depending on the nature exiled from Shadow Providence. Then where will you and whomever you are protecting be? Is that what you want?"

He jerked his head back in surprise with such force she was amazed it was still attached. "No, but what you're asking…"

Nightmare strolled up beside her. "You're risking her life by withholding information that in itself is punishable by death."

"They wouldn't hurt them."

*There's more than one.* "Windwalker, Storm, take him to one of the cells in the basement."

"Wait, my Queen." Winter Thaw stood, the air around them cooling as his control frizzled. "Send them away and I'll tell you."

She nodded and Windwalker and Storm stepped back into the house. "This is your last chance."

"My sister Snow and her son Jack. Snow's husband refused to serve Queen Lisa, and in a fit she blew up the house, with the plan to kill everyone inside. Snow was pregnant with Jack then and managed to escape. She hid in my cabin. It was weeks before I found her there. I thought she had died, so when I found her alive I refused to let anyone harm her. They live there, causing no harm to anyone, and everyone thinks they are dead. Please, my Queen, Snow and her son are innocent."

Part of her hated that everyone feared her because of her title, but the other part knew it would be one of the keys to keep her safe. If people thought she was willing to kill without reason they would think twice before attacking her. "I know some Queens are vindictive, and will use any reason to strike out on those below them, those who cannot protect themselves. But I'm not one of those Queens. I'll protect those in my land as they protect me. I want to meet her, take me to her, and we'll figure out something to keep her and the child safe."

"Yes, my Queen." He seemed reserved to the fact there was nothing he could do to get out of the predicament he was in without committing himself to the dungeon.

The trek through the woods with only Nightmare and Dreamer as her Enforcers was not how Kayla had expected to spend the day. The other

guards weren't pleased Nightmare would risk taking her out without more Enforcers after the attacks last night, but when she told then if anyone had a problem with it they could be on grounds duty for a month instead of guarding her, they quieted down.

"How much farther, Winter Thaw?"

"You'll see where you come into my land, just around the bend." The bend was a good twenty feet before them but she realized what he meant when she rounded it. The forest was covered in snow and ice, looking like a winter wonderland, causing Nightmare's earlier words to come flooding back. *He has the ability to thaw ice under your feet only to refreeze it with you on the other side.*

Nightmare turned his head to the side to look at Winter Thaw. "Clear a path to the cabin, the Queen does not need to slip on an ice patch and break a leg."

"I promise it's not as slick as it might look."

"Clear a path or the Queen goes no farther and you know your fate." Nightmare slipped his arm from Kayla's grasp as if concerned they'd have a problem.

"Very well." A clear dirt path began to appear before them. "It will close behind you as protection. You never know who's lurking in the woods."

It was another fifteen minutes of walking through the cold winter air before the cabin came into view. "Finally." She signed, happy to be done trekking through the woods. *What was I thinking?*

Winter Thaw slipped in front of them, grabbing hold of the door handle. "Snow?" He called out when he saw no one.

"Winter Thaw, where is she? If this is a trap I'll personally kill you." Nightmare's hand went to his gun as he stepped in front of her. Dreamer moved closer, his hand on his sword ready to draw it if necessary.

"She's here. She might have seen us coming. Just give me a moment."

He walked farther into the cabin, and knelt near the table. Reaching under the table he opened a trap door. "Snow, come out. I promise no one's here to harm you."

Nightmare stepped closer to the opening, looking down inside. "Your brother has risked much to bring us here. Come out."

Timidly a terrified woman crept up the stairs, a small sleeping child curled in her arms. "Please...don't hurt my son."

Kayla stepped away from Dreamer, but she kept Nightmare in front of her. "I'm not here to hurt either of you. I'm here to help."

"Snow, this is Queen Kayla, the new ruler of Storm Hollow. She means you no harm."

"Why don't you put the boy down, I'm sure he's getting heavy and we can talk." When Snow's gaze darted to her guards. "Nightmare and Dreamer are only here for my protection, not to harm you, your son, or Winter Thaw."

"I wouldn't have brought them here if I wasn't positive it's safe," Winter Thaw urged. "I promised I'd keep you safe and I never go back on my word. Now sit and talk to our Queen, and I'll put him to bed." He took his nephew from her arms and even though she held tight for a moment, she did let him take the boy.

"Why are you here?"

"I asked your brother to be one of my Enforcers, but I needed him to tell me who he's hiding; I needed for there to be no secrets. He had to come clean about your situation in order to gain his position. I'm just here to help you. You can't live like this, it's not fit to raise a child so far from everyone."

"How dare you tell me how to raise my child!"

"Snow," Winter Thaw scolded, coming back into the main living area of the cabin. "Remember your place and who you're talking to."

Kayla held up her hand stopping Winter Thaw. "I'm just saying he needs a home where he's not hidden away. He needs interactions with both children his own age and adults. He's young now but he won't stay that way. You want him to grow into a happy and healthy boy, don't you? Let me help you."

"How can you help me? Queen Lisa will kill me if she finds out I'm still alive." Snow collapsed into the chair, sobs wracking body.

Kayla crept toward the chair, careful not to make any sudden movements. "No, she can't. I've taken over Storm Hollow, she has no claim here any longer. Come back to town with us I'll see that you're protected."

"There's a cottage on the outskirts of the main compound," Nightmare began. "It was used as a house for visiting parties for years, but now it's abandoned. If our Queen agrees, you could turn it into a home for you, your son, and Winter Thaw until you're comfortable returning to town completely." He looked to Kayla, as if he was unsure he should have mentioned the cottage.

"That's a great idea." Kayla beamed. "There's a pool on the grounds, you can teach Jack how to swim. You can make a true home for you and your son. You'll be safe there."

"Snow, take the offer," Winter Thaw urged softly. "Queen Kayla is a reasonable Queen, and she'll bring many changes to our land. I want to help her in any way I can to bring to life the future of the Stormkins—the one so many prophesied about. I didn't believe it then, but I believe it now. I want you to be a part of it with me. If you won't do it for me, do it for Jack. He can't live like this forever, it will turn him rogue." He knelt in front of her, taking her hand in his. "I wouldn't have brought them here if I didn't believe you'd be safe. I won't let anything happened to you or Jack."

"You can offer her protection…I have nothing to offer." Tears slid down Snow's cheeks.

"You can heal. There isn't a Queen who would turn away an additional healer." Winter Thaw used his index finger to raise her chin, making her look up at them.

"You're a healer, in the natural sense?" Nightmare took a step forward, his voice even and unthreatening.

It was clear he made her fearful, so Kayla leaned forward, bringing the attention away from him, and tried again. "Snow, look at me. Are you a true healer who can heal by touch?"

"Yes."

She nodded, and turned to Nightmare. "Give me your knife."

"My Queen?" he asked, but unstrapped it from his belt and handed it to her.

She didn't answer, just took hold of the knife and slit a small cut in her thumb. Blood dripped down her hand, pooling in her palm. "Heal me."

"My Queen, you shouldn't have done that. Your blood is special, it should not be spilled to prove a point, especially not when there are others around you could have used." Snow's voice held a hint of surprise.

"I'm not that type of Queen. I won't risk others when I'm not willing to risk myself. Heal it and there won't be any more wasted blood."

Snow reached her hand out slowly as if afraid the Enforcers would attack for touching her. With a final look to Winter Thaw, she cupped her hand over Kayla's bleeding thumb.

A warm glowing sensation surrounded her hand, as though she held it to an open flame. There was no pain, but the heat made her gasp in surprise. When Snow took her hand away, Kayla's thumb was healed, leaving behind no scar or even any sign there had been a wound there at all.

Nightmare looked down at Kayla's outstretched thumb before looking to Snow again. "The Queen's looking for a healer, come back with us and take the position."

"What of Starr? Is she no longer in Storm Hollow."

"As of now she's still in Storm Hollow, but she won't be seeing to the Queen any longer. We had plans to seek out a new healer at the next council meeting, but this is an ideal situation for both parties."

"Nightmare's right. Come back with us." Kayla scooted the chair closer to Snow, but still far enough away that she wouldn't scare her. She was like an abused dog, scared and unsure of her surroundings. Everyone around her was moving on egg shells, afraid what might happen if she was startled.

Snow looked at Winter Thaw before turning back to Kayla. "Okay."

# Chapter Thirty-Eight

Stretched out on one of the patio lounge chairs, Kayla sat with a glass of hurricane in hand as she watched Dreamer run through weapons training with a handful of new ground Enforcers. Dreamer was coming into his role as Lieutenant Enforcer better than she could have expected. He was flourishing and his confidence was growing with each passing day.

The main compound's population expanded. She and Nightmare discussed the possibility of a training school for Enforcer potentials.

Even with the increased activity in the main compound, she still kept the main house as her own home with only Nightmare, Dreamer, and the house staff living there with her. With the new center of command being erected, soon she would no longer conduct meetings in the main house. The new building would keep only the selected elite Enforcers outside the walls of her private home.

"More hurricane my Queen?" Sitting next to her, Nightmare held a bottle in his hand ready to pour more into her glass.

She frowned at *my Queen*. She still had to remind Nightmare and Dreamer to call her Kayla, but centuries of training and custom were hard to break. "No, thanks."

No matter what they called her she knew how they felt about her. They proved their commitment to protecting her every day, and their commitment to her in other ways each night. Well, every other night since they rotated most nights. Some nights she'd convince them just to snuggle with her; she enjoyed the warmth of their bodies as she slept, surrounded by security.

With the threats surrounding them daily and the upcoming council meeting, which had her stomach in knots, she wanted all the comfort she could find. Her men gave her that, and more. Nightmare and Dreamer had become her port in a sea of rough waves, but with each passing day her sea legs grew stronger.

She had no idea if she really was all that the prophecies said she would be. Everything in her life had turned upside down in a few short weeks. But she wouldn't trade it—any of it—for anything else.

Lifting her glass, she toasted her new life—Kayla, Queen of Storm Hollow.

*May I always live in interesting times…*

# Marissa Dobson

Born and raised in the Pittsburgh, Pennsylvania area, Marissa Dobson now resides about an hour from Washington, D.C. She's a lady who likes to keep busy, and is always busy doing something. With two different college degrees, she believes you're never done learning.

Being the first daughter to an avid reader, this gave her the advantage of learning to read at a young age. Since learning to read she has always had her nose in a book. It wasn't until she was a teenager that she started writing down the stories she came up with.

Marissa is blessed with a wonderful supportive husband, Thomas. He's her other half and allows her to stay home and pursue her writing. He puts up with all her quirks and listens to her brainstorm in the middle of the night.

Her writing buddy Pup Cameron, a cocker spaniel, is always around to listen to her bounce ideas off him. He might not be able to answer, but he's helpful in his own ways.

She loves to hear from readers so send her an email at marissa@marissadobson.com or visit her online at http://www.marissadobson.com.

# Other Books by Marissa Dobson

**Alaskan Tigers:**

Tiger Time

The Tiger's Heart

Tigress for Two

Night with a Tiger

Trusting a Tiger

Alaskan Tigers Box Set Vol. 1

Jinx's Mate

Two for Protection

Bearing Secrets

Tiger Tracks

Healing the Clan

Alaskan Tigers Box Set Vol. 2

Her Black Tiger

Tiger Trouble

**Forever Creek Shifters:**

Forever's Fight

Protecting Forever

**Stormkin:**

Storm Queen

**Crimson Hollow:**

Romancing the Fox

Loving the Bears

A Lion's Chance

Swift Move

Purrable Lion

Bearly Alive

Saved by a Lion

Furever Mated Box Set

**Reaper:**

A Touch of Death

**SEALed for You:**

Ace in the Hole

Explosive Passion

Operation Family

**Marine for You:**

Lucky Chance

Back from Hell

A Marine's Second Chance

**Tanner Cycles:**

Until Sydney

**Phantom Security:**

Different Sides

Undercover Agent

**Cedar Grove Medical:**

Hope's Toy Chest

Destiny's Wish

Leena's Dream

**Fate:**

Snowy Fate

Sarah's Fate

Mason's Fate

As Fate Would Have It

**Half Moon Harbor Resort:**

Learning to Live

Learning What Love Is

Her Cowboy's Heart

Half Moon Harbor Box Set

**Beyond Monogamy:**

Theirs to Treasure

**Clearwater:**

Winterbloom

Unexpected Forever

Losing to Win

Christmas Countdown

The Surrogate

Clearwater Romance Vol. 1

Small Town Doctor

**Stand Alone:**

Through Smoke

SEALed Rescue

SEALed in Texas

Starting Over

Secret Valentine

Restoring Love